A Candlelight Ecstasy Romance®

**"BRENDAN . . ." SHE WHISPERED,
AND AS HIS NAME ESCAPED
HER THOROUGHLY KISSED LIPS,
SHE CAME TO HER SENSES.**

"We won't let this happen again. I mean . . . I
didn't expect this from myself."

"Really?" Brendan's eyes probed hers.

"Well," she said lightly, "it's not every day that
I'm kissed by a famous race car driver."

"Nor have I ever been kissed by an up-and-coming investigative reporter who is also a social butterfly."

"One party at Roulette makes me a social butterfly?" Lisa asked incredulously.

"No, but certainly the company you keep tells
me that you're no stranger to New York night life."

"You mean Steve Hanley? He happens to be an
old friend, Mr. Donovan," she snapped, then
added, "and how I spend my evenings, and with
whom, has no bearing on my job as a journalist.
Now, shall we call it a night?"

CANDLELIGHT ECSTASY ROMANCES®

RIVER RAPTURE

Patricia Markham

A CANDLELIGHT ECSTASY ROMANCE®

Published by
Dell Publishing Co., Inc.
1 Dag Hammarskjold Plaza
New York, New York 10017

Dell ® TM 681510, Dell Publishing Co., Inc.

Candlelight Ecstasy Romance®, 1,203,540, is a registered
trademark of
Dell Publishing Co., Inc., New York, New York.

ISBN: 0-440-17453-8

Printed in the United States of America

First printing—October 1984

To Our Readers:

We have been delighted with your enthusiastic response to Candlelight Ecstasy Romances®, and we thank you for the interest you have shown in this exciting series.

In the upcoming months we will continue to present the distinctive, sensuous love stories you have come to expect only from Ecstasy. We look forward to bringing you many more books from your favorite authors and also the very finest work from new authors of contemporary romantic fiction.

As always, we are striving to present the unique, absorbing love stories that you enjoy most—books that are more than ordinary romance.

Your suggestions and comments are always welcome. Please write to us at the address below.

Sincerely,

The Editors
Candlelight Romances
1 Dag Hammarskjold Plaza
New York, New York 10017

CHAPTER ONE

Clack-clack. Clack-clack. Ping!

Lisa Taylor allowed herself a quick smile of satisfaction and tugged at the sheet of white paper in her typewriter. It was the last page of an article due by 5:00 P.M. today at *Lifestyle* magazine.

Old Maish Lawrence, the subject of the profile, could never complain that she hadn't put enough effort into the piece, she thought. Only that she had probed deeply enough to discover that he owned half of Manhattan without anybody ever knowing it. Until now.

Lisa smiled again, broader this time. The L. B. Taylor byline was beginning to open doors for her, leading to more and more article assignments. In the past three years she had published a number of features on such diverse topics as preschool education, home entertaining, and midlife career changes, plus a few profiles on offbeat Manhattanites. Her next subject, Brendan Donovan, was her first celebrity profile, which might be difficult to do since he could be hard to pin down in the eight weeks until her article was due at *Lifestyle*.

With a start, Lisa swiveled in her chair to stare at the portable television perched on her kitchen counter. She always left it on as background noise while she was working. And now the announcer's voice had cut through her senses, matching her thoughts.

Brendan Donovan. Lisa didn't believe in mental telepa-

9

thy, but it did seem as though her unspoken words had somehow connected with the image now on the television screen, becoming one and the same.

Sports Today, which appeared every weekday preceding the game shows, was covering auto racing on this five-minute segment. Lisa listened closely, furrowing her brows in concentration.

Today's Grand Prix race featured a winner . . . and a question. Tony Traverti the winner . . . Brendan Donovan the man in question. Since he abruptly retired following the fiery crash last year that involved his friend and foe, Guy Tremaine, Donovan has been conspicuously absent from the racing scene.

This past weekend, however, he returned to the race world at Madrid, Spain . . . if only as a spectator. Several of his close acquaintances, however, were heard to speculate that Donovan, the world champion just two years ago, would return to race again. Sports Today *is following the story, ready to report to you the moment we have confirmation or denial of these reports. . . .*

Lisa grabbed her pencil and jotted several key words in her notebook. The Brendan Donovan piece was looking more intriguing all the time. Not only was he "the man every woman wants," as *Lifestyle* editor Marge Kent had described him, but he appeared to have a knack for getting media attention as well.

Lisa wondered if Donovan was one of those publicity-seeking types who was happy only if his face and name were plastered on a million magazine covers. Like Steve Hanley. Lisa tossed her tawny head, as if that small action could erase the pain of a love affair lost.

Lisa rose and snapped off the television. Conscious once again of her deadline, she hurried into her bedroom to change clothes for the trip to the magazine's offices. Her bare feet made no sound on the deep plum-colored

10

carpeting as she opened her closet to grab an aquamarine shirtwaist dress from the rack.

She slipped it over her head, enjoying the feel of silk on her skin. Jeans and denim work shirt were perfectly acceptable attire for a free-lance writer, Lisa knew, but only in the privacy of her apartment. *Lifestyle* expected a well-dressed, put-together type who was professional right down to the alligator heels Lisa stepped into.

She paused at the mirror over her dresser and quickly ran a brush through her thick, shoulder-length hair, which nearly matched the blond wood grain of her furniture. "A tigress's hair," Steve had called it.

Lisa dabbed a touch of lipstick to a face that glowed with good health and energy. The magazine's staffers always remarked that Lisa looked like she'd stepped out of a vitamin advertisement.

"Health, if not happiness," she said flippantly to her reflection. A pretty woman in aquamarine silk with blue eyes to match stared back at her, as if in reproach. As if to say, "Lisa Taylor, you're on your way to achieving your career goals. Does it matter so terribly much that your personal life hasn't met with the same roaring success?"

Not so much, Lisa reflected . . . only when she saw Steve's name linked to this model or that actress. At those times she would ache for the nearness of him. Now that she had achieved the first hints of success, she wanted someone to share it all with.

The clock on her nightstand read 4:05, Lisa realized with a start. There was barely time to get to the midtown office, if she hurried. She stuffed her article into her leather briefcase on her way out the door of her Greenwich Village brownstone.

Having successfully hailed a cab—not a small feat in New York City—Lisa gazed out through its windows at the city she had adopted. Teeming with life, with people

11

who spelled its past and future, the city never failed to energize her. True, she visited Long Island on frequent weekend trips with friends just to escape the crowds, but the city was her lifeline.

It hadn't always been so. Until she was seven years old she had lived in Cincinnati, Ohio. But after the deaths of her mother and father in a car crash, she had been left in the care of her Aunt Phyllis and Uncle Bertram.

Her aunt and uncle had no children of their own, and the outdoor adventures of Lisa's early youth had given way to rather regimented activities that hadn't much to do with climbing trees or skipping stones across a muddy creek. Little girls weren't supposed to get their hands dirty, Aunt Phyllis reminded her.

Lisa had learned to play the piano and to wear frilly pink dresses that scratched your skin if you so much as swung your feet. Consequently, by the time she won a scholarship to college and moved away from her aunt and uncle's house, Lisa was content to leave sports and the great outdoors to more adventurous types. Instead, she concentrated on her journalism classes.

Now, in New York, Lisa reflected that her enthusiasm for the city had really come to her aid in the Maish Lawrence profile tucked in her briefcase. In her determination to get to know Manhattan, she had explored its treasures each day until her feet ached. The result, in addition to a closetful of well-worn loafers, was a valuable familiarity with the city. She'd had to use nearly every resource—City Hall, the mayor's office, the stacks in the main library—to come up with the story. She probably couldn't survive even a day in the wilderness, Lisa decided, but she was tough to beat in the concrete jungle.

She arrived at *Lifestyle* to find that Marge Kent, her articles editor and friend, was tied up in an emergency conference. Lisa left the Lawrence article with Marge's secretary and rode the elevator to the lobby. She toyed with the idea of a Bloomingdale's shopping expedition.

Lisa had several hours before she had to get ready for the evening. A party at Roulette was on tonight's agenda. *Lifestyle* was sponsoring this private party, and although Lisa would have preferred a no-pressure evening curled up with a good Perry Mason mystery, she knew her absence would be noticed.

Marge Kent had attached a note to the invitation that arrived several weeks ago, hinting strongly that Lisa should attend come hell or high water. *You will be most interested in the guest list,* Marge had written. *I assure you.*

Lisa sent in her RSVP card with a check mark penciled in the "yes" box. At the time, she had looked forward to the party, but now she had mixed feelings. Writing an article under deadline pressure was no easy task, and the completion of the Maish Lawrence piece had drained her mentally. Physically, she could handle a shopping expedition on Lexington Avenue, but she wasn't sure she was up to meeting new people tonight at Roulette.

However, the decision was already made. And she needed a bracelet to go with her new dress. While she was at it, she decided, she had better stock up on a few clothing items she would need for next week's interview sessions with Brendan Donovan in South Carolina.

She headed on foot toward Bloomie's, mentally reviewing the contents of her closet. Just about everything she owned was suitable for trudging around the city—given a choice between walking and riding, she always chose the former—but what was right for New York City seemed a little too somber for Hilton Head Island, South Carolina.

Inside Bloomingdale's, she located her favorite saleswoman on the third floor and happily spent the next two hours trying on clothes that reminded her of ocean

13

breezes and blessed sunshine. She settled on a yellow tunic-and-trousers outfit, on sale because it was part of last season's collection, and some less expensive knit tops and shorts. She bought a sundress that was ridiculously expensive for the amount of material it contained; its redeeming and altogether irresistible feature was that it was red and white and Lisa knew it would look smashing against tanned skin.

On her way out, the first-floor jewelry department claimed her attention. She spotted a simple silver bracelet that would go perfectly with the dress she was wearing to the Roulette party. While the clerk was ringing up the sale, her glance fell on a bracelet beneath the protective cover of the glass counter in front of her. It was of the most delicate pink, made of tiny polished stones linked together by pearls. She had one just like it, tucked away in the bottom of her dresser drawer. She never wore it anymore.

Steve had given it to her, three months after they started dating. He had had to cancel a planned date to a concert at Radio City Music Hall; relatives had unexpectedly arrived from out of town, he had told her. She found out later that he had lied. A friend had seen him and Angela Moore, debutante-of-the-year a few years back, dining cozily at Elaine's, a trendy East Side restaurant. That had been the beginning of the end for them, though she didn't know it then. The bracelet in her drawer was a reminder—not, as Steve intended it, of his love, but of his infidelity.

Suddenly she couldn't wait to escape the clamor of Bloomingdale's.

Lisa stood in the shower, letting the hot jet spray of water hit her skin with invigorating force. Steam rose around her, clouding her in its cocoon of smothering warmth. Her hands gently soaped her lean, supple body. Her thoughts returned, unbidden, to Steve.

She remembered their first meeting. Her apartment neighbors, a middle-aged couple, had invited her to a housewarming party for their new country home in Connecticut. Lisa had arrived at Linda and Ron's place with a chilled bottle of Beaujolais and was immediately engulfed in a crowd of fifty or so well-wishers.

A man had appeared at her side. "Do you really intend to give this to our hosts . . . or maybe you'll reconsider and share it with me?" He laughed and Lisa laughed with him, gently insisting that the wine should definitely find its way to Linda and Ron's pantry.

His name was Steve, he told her. He knew the hosts through mutual friends. And, like her, he was not a native New Yorker. He had grown up in California.

Steve asked about her and her work. She gave him a sketchy outline and was about to ask about his occupation when a gray-haired man approached, slapping Steve's back in a familiar way. At the same time, Linda, in the doorway to the kitchen, signaled Lisa with a slightly frantic wave.

Lisa made her way through the crowd. Linda whispered, "What a lifesaver you are, Lisa dear. Remember the artichoke casserole you fixed for us in your apartment last winter? I've tried to re-create it here and it's . . . well . . . it's not doing what yours did. It doesn't even look edible at this point!" Linda's expression was a mixture of despair and hope.

"I'll take a look," Lisa assured her, and followed her into the kitchen. Within minutes she had rescued the casserole with a generous helping of mayonnaise. When she reappeared in the living room, Steve had been joined by a tall, gorgeous redhead.

So much for that little encounter, Lisa thought. She joined a group in the small library and spent the next several hours in earnest discussion of the "new" journalism that was catching on throughout the country. When it came time to leave to catch a ride back to the city, she involuntarily scanned the living room for Steve. He was gone. So was the redheaded woman.

Two days later she received a half-dozen yellow roses from the city's best-known floral shop. *To the girl who rescued the artichoke casserole,* the note read. A sweet gesture for Linda to make, Lisa thought. She turned the card over and read, *Mind if I call you? Steve.*

She had laughed softly to herself. She must have made a stronger impression than she'd credited herself for. That evening, Steve had called. His last name failed to register fully. They went to dinner the following night. It was then that she had learned he was Steve Hanley, the professional baseball player. She also learned that she was vulnerable to his charm. Steve Hanley, it seemed, had swept her off her feet.

Lisa shook her head thoroughly in the shower. Water flew about her face and coursed down her throat and breasts in tiny rivulets. She winced, not sure if it was from the hot water or the memory of him. She reached up to turn off the shower spigot.

Gingerly she stepped onto the cool white bath tiles and reached for a fluffy apricot towel. Lisa wrapped herself in its soft folds, hugging it to her body.

In the bedroom, her glance fell on her assignment folder. Work, she decided, would fill the time until she had to leave. She hoped it would fill her mind as well, to take her away from the past and the pain.

For the next two hours she read about Brendan Donovan. Her folder was filled with newspapers and magazine clippings. There were a few grainy photographs that revealed a man with the sort of uncharacteristic looks many women found irresistible. Lisa happened not to be one of them. Cold, calculating types who drove race cars

16

for a living were not her cup of tea. A ridiculous thought, she chided herself. This was no time to let personal bias get in the way of her professionalism.

She took notes, some detailed, some just random, and then let her mind rest on the enigma that was Mr. Donovan. Here was an extremely daring man who apparently now lived a rather tame life by comparison. Despite the media coverage, he was an extremely private man who granted few interviews. Why her? Lisa wondered. Why the *Lifestyle* piece? She meant to discover his motives once she met him.

Glancing at the clock, she uncurled her legs from the chair in her bedroom. It was time to get ready for the party.

Lisa reached in the closet for the white knit, high-necked, long-sleeved dress that did little to hide her curves. It shimmered when the light struck its minuscule silver threads, and the new silver bracelet she had purchased today complemented it perfectly.

Lisa smoothed the dress over her body and took a critical look at herself in the mirror, thinking she had to do something with her hair. She usually let it fall free, but this dress, she decided, deserved something more. With several quick brushstrokes she swept her hair up away from her face and neck, and gathered it in soft, radiant waves, pinning it with a silver haircomb.

She picked up her evening bag, retrieved her wrap from the hall closet, and shut her front door behind her.

The taxi deposited her under the canopied entryway of Roulette. Marge Kent was just inside, heading for the elevator as Lisa rushed up to join her.

Roulette, the newest "in" spot for the New York nightclub crowd, was teeming with excitement. Flashing lights and the pounding, insistent beat of rock music assaulted the pair as they stepped inside, having risen fifty-six stories to arrive on the skyscraper's top floor. They were led to a private, discreetly roped-off area of the club that had been reserved for the party. Marge promised, "Be right back," and headed for the bar.

Lisa shrugged off her wrap and draped it over a chair.

"Lisa!"

She froze. It couldn't be, but it was.

Steve Hanley wrapped her five feet six frame in a bear hug, as though they were the best of friends, not former lovers who hadn't spoken for eight months.

"Steve. It's good to see you." Her voice came out breathless, as though he had knocked the wind out of her. Which, of course, he had. Her words were the truth and a lie. It *was* good to see his familiar face with the all-American good looks, the slightly crooked grin . . . even the little cowlick that he still tried and failed to make disappear. What wasn't good, she knew, was the aching feeling that enveloped her heart. You're *over* him, she reminded herself. But somehow the words failed to find their way to tell her emotions.

Had she willed him to appear? Seeing the bracelet in Bloomingdale's . . . had that been an omen?

His eyes sought hers in the old, familiar way. "I kind of thought you might be here tonight. So I wangled an invitation."

She smiled in spite of herself. "That sounds like the Steve Hanley I know. . . ."

He grabbed her arm lightly. "Come along to the bar with me and pick your favorite poison. We've got some catching up to do. Did you hear, there's talk I might be traded to San Diego?"

Your life, *your* career, Lisa thought, not mine. Never mine. And it was just like Steve to assume that she would want to spend the evening with him. He had an infuriating habit of making decisions for other people, she remembered, including her. Well, this was *now,* not a year

18

ago, and she wouldn't meekly follow his commands. Nothing good would come of this reunion, she knew.

"I'm afraid I'm not one of those who believe in 'for old times' sake,' " she said soberly, matching his look.

"I've changed, Lisa, really." Steve was uncharacteristically serious. The cocky smile was gone, replaced by an expression of need so genuine that Lisa was forced to listen despite her misgivings.

"The old Steve Hanley is gone," he was telling her. "Something happened to me right after you left . . . it's too complicated to tell you now, above all this noise."

His grip tightened on her arm. "Have just one drink with me, Lisa. Please?"

She told herself she wasn't taken in by him. He had gone through these "changes" before, she reminded herself.

He chucked her lightly on the chin. "C'mon, Lisa. I'm probably the only guy here who knows you order a vodka collins without the vodka."

She had to laugh. He knew so many of her little secrets. But he didn't know everything.

"I can hold my liquor just a little better now. I drink gin and tonics . . . *with* the gin."

Without her even noticing, he had steered her toward the bar, she realized. Okay, she would talk to him tonight, if he was so determined. But that would be the end of it.

She touched him lightly on the sleeve of his tuxedo jacket. "There can't be an 'us' anymore, Steve. You do know that." If he heard her above the din, he gave no sign. He was already ordering their drinks.

Back at the table, Steve filled her in on the latest contract negotiations between his ball club and his agent . . . who, it turned out, had been the one who told Steve about the Roulette party tonight. Freddy Ames, the agent, was supposed to be here also, Steve told Lisa. And what had she been doing with herself?

Lisa gave him the barest details of her work, and was surprised to see him actually pay attention to her words. While they were dating, Lisa's career had been barely of interest to Steve. He had condescendingly viewed her writing as a mere pastime, something with which she filled her days until the right man came along.

Lisa sensed a growing respect from him now as she related news about the article she had just completed. Perhaps he *had* changed.

A waiter came to the table and Steve ordered another drink for himself; Lisa's was still half finished. And then he spotted Freddy Ames among the crowd and called over to him.

Lisa hadn't liked Freddy when she first met him and she'd liked him even less when she got to know him. Middle-aged, with the pasty complexion of a man who spent his life doing business in smoke-filled bars, Freddy made his way over to their table. Trailing in his wake were three women who looked barely old enough to be drinking the margaritas they balanced in their hands.

Introductions were made, but Lisa caught only a fraction of the names amid the din of music and laughter. She ordered another gin and tonic when the waiter brought Steve's drink. Perhaps, she thought, the gin would make it easier to mingle with or without Steve. It was funny, but she had no problem talking to strangers when she was a journalist on assignment. But here, in a social situation such as tonight's, her natural friendliness and ease abandoned her. No words tumbled forth, and her smile seemed to take all the effort she could muster.

The conversation, or what could pass for conversation in the raucous surroundings, flowed around her. The talk focused on percentages and personal-appearance fees. The discussion of which celebrities were most in demand had nothing to do with Lisa Taylor. So she turned her attention instead to the scene around her.

Couples gyrated to the pulsating music coming from the club's elaborate multispeaker sound system. A curly-headed deejay urged more dancers to the floor as he flipped a switch for the next album. Lisa couldn't fathom how one more body could be squeezed into the dime-size circle of brass and mirrors that served as a dance floor, but couple after couple nevertheless joined the dancers already on the floor.

Lisa watched a girl she recognized as a *Lifestyle* staffer. She was clad in voluminous, gauzy red trousers and a purple-satin quilted vest, and she moved in rhythm with her partner, who wore a costume of star-studded khaki shorts and shirt. Her own dress, Lisa thought, no doubt seemed drab and uninspired to the uninhibited regulars of the club. Well, she was not a Roulette regular and had no intention of becoming one. The dress was *her* and she was glad it did not scream for attention in this glitzy crowd.

Lisa glanced at Steve. He was still involved in his conversation and didn't look up at her. He had ordered another martini, too. She noticed one of the girls at the table, who could have been Raquel Welch's sister, flick his gold cigarette lighter as though it was just one of many possessions of his she was quite familiar with. Lisa told herself not to be surprised. Steve was Steve, after all. Which was exactly why she wasn't going to do any more "catching up" with him. She would seek out Marge and her friends.

She gathered her clutch purse from the table and was about to say her good-byes to the group when she felt a hand touch her shoulder. A man's voice from behind her ear said, "No one should leave Roulette without dancing at least once."

She turned quickly, startled, and looked into eyes that

21

were the color of deep chocolate, warm and melting right into her own.

"Will you dance with me?"

She nodded, slowly, as if her mind were on an electric current that had malfunctioned due to a power failure. There was a slow-motion quality to her movements, too, as she rose to her feet. She looked over to where Steve was sitting. He was gone.

The deejay had shifted to a mellow mood, and the easy, soulful velvet that was Roberta Flack's voice filled the club. The stranger led her toward the dance floor.

No, not a stranger, her brain told her. From the corner of her eye she regarded his profile as he guided her to an open spot on the dance floor. Thick brown hair was cut close to his head, but not so close that there wasn't evidence of stubborn, springy curls. In the dim light of Roulette she saw that he possessed the kind of tan that comes with the life of a sun-worshiper.

His arm circled her waist and she felt herself succumb to its seductive curve. *Why do I feel as if I could dance all night with him?* He held her close, his smooth, chiseled cheek resting ever so lightly on her hair. She breathed in the nearness of him, and was reminded somehow of the woods near her childhood home in Ohio.

Everything about him reminded her of something, she thought. *Have I seen him somewhere before? Those eyes . . .*

Lisa stiffened. He couldn't be, she thought. *Could he?*

"Something wrong?" He held her slightly away, and was looking at her with an expression that was half amused, half serious. She stared back at him.

"N-no," she faltered. She leaned into his arms again, and they stepped in tandem to the soothing music.

Nothing was wrong, she amended silently to herself, yet nothing was right. The man whose arms held her was Brendan Donovan.

CHAPTER TWO

Her cheeks flamed with embarrassment. *Brendan Donovan,* she thought, *and here I am acting like a silly school-girl with a crush.* She closed her eyes and rested her head against his tuxedo jacket. She needed time to collect herself.

One of the cardinal rules of journalism, Lisa reminded herself, was to maintain an emotional distance from one's subject. Yet Lisa knew that she had already bridged that distance. In this man's arms, she had forgotten that a world of editors and sources and deadline pressure even existed. Brendan Donovan, without even trying, had awakened the woman inside her.

"You dance very well," he whispered through her hair.

She looked up at him with a wry smile. "And you, Mr. Donovan, are threatening my reputation."

"Am I, Miss L. B. Taylor? I hardly think that's possible from what Marge Kent told me when she pointed you out to me. And since when is the simple pleasure of dancing denied a beautiful woman like you?"

Her cheeks dimpled despite her best efforts. "In case you've forgotten . . ."

"Quite the opposite. I'm looking forward to our interview. Tell me, Miss Taylor, have you danced with any of your other interview subjects?"

"They've never asked," Lisa replied lightly.

"Their loss," he complimented her.

23

They danced to the music without speaking for a moment.

"Have you been writing for *Lifestyle* long?" Brendan asked then.

"Several years," Lisa answered.

"And what famous closets have you found skeletons in?"

"None, really," Lisa told him. "My articles have dealt more with everyday things . . . mothers of young children who can't find quality day-care, for instance. And I once wrote about a Princeton economics professor who decided in the middle of class one day that what he really wanted to do with his life was move to Kentucky and be a chair caner."

She glanced up at him. "In fact, Mr. Donovan, you're my first celebrity assignment."

"Hmmm" was all he said.

Funny, Lisa thought, how a murmured "hmmm" could dash one's self-confidence. Brendan Donovan didn't sound too thrilled at the prospect of being the instrument of her big break.

Brendan spoke again. "I understand you're Bertram Taylor's niece."

"That's right." Now how on earth, Lisa thought, would he know that?

He answered her unspoken question. "I have a friend in the brokerage business who knows your uncle." Bertram Taylor was chairman of the board of one of the largest brokerage firms in the country. When people found out who her uncle was, they inevitably assumed that she was pampered and wealthy. Although she *had* been fortunate enough to have had a very comfortable childhood, Lisa was very much on her own now. By her choice, not her aunt and uncle's. In fact, they were rather embarrassed that she chose to live on her salary alone.

But Brendan Donovan, who apparently thought his

detective work had told him what he needed to know, wasn't aware of her independent streak.

That's fine, Lisa thought. *He needn't know everything about me.*

"Uncle Bertram is like a father to me," she told Brendan. Flippantly, she added, "What else do you know about me?"

Brendan leaned back and gazed down into her eyes. She had to remind herself to follow his dance lead, so paralyzing was the effect of his eyes on hers.

"That you're beautiful . . . charming . . . you dance very well. . . ."

"Because I go to parties every evening where handsome strangers ask me to dance." She laughed.

"I shouldn't be surprised," he said somberly.

"Actually—" she began.

"Hush." He placed two firm fingers against her lips. "You'll have more than enough time to tell me next week. But now is the time for music, not words. Relax. . . ."

His hand caressed her head, pressing it against his shoulder once more.

Lisa gave herself to the moment. She moved to his lead, and they swept along the dance floor as though each knew where the other wished to go. Lisa felt the warmth of Brendan's chest through the thick white cotton of his shirt. Was that his heart beating in tandem with her own?

Roberta Flack's voice ebbed as the music came to an end.

Lisa disengaged herself from Brendan's arms. She did not trust herself to look at him as they made their way back to her table, his hand on her elbow to guide her.

Steve reappeared suddenly before them. His expression toward Brendan was decidedly unfriendly. Lisa thought he was about to say something unkind, when Marge hastily intervened.

"I see you two have met," Marge said. Trust Marge,

25

Lisa thought gratefully, to appear on the scene in the nick of time.

Marge continued. "But Brendan, I don't think you've met Lisa's . . . uh . . . friend, Steve Hanley."

The two men shook hands somewhat guardedly, Lisa thought, like two prizefighters matching gloves before the first round.

She said to Steve, "Mr. Donovan has agreed to be my next interview subject for *Lifestyle.*"

The name registered with Steve. "You're the race car driver? Grand Prix?"

"*Ex*-driver," replied Brendan. "Those days are over for me."

He said it with no trace of rancor or bitterness, but Lisa thought she detected a flicker of—what?—regret or sadness or something indefinable in the depths of his brown eyes.

A smile, revealing strong, even white teeth, replaced whatever she thought she had seen. "I am not what you would call a baseball fanatic, but I believe you're to be congratulated, Mr. Hanley. Most Valuable Player in the play-offs, weren't you?"

Steve beamed, pleased at the recognition. "Modesty begs that I remind you that the other team won, unfortunately."

Brendan glanced at Lisa and then back at Steve. "I would say you're recovering quite nicely. Miss Taylor would make any man forget even the most serious troubles. She had that effect on me, in just one dance." He smiled briefly. "If you'll excuse me?"

With a nod at Steve, he turned to Lisa and took her hand. "Until next week?" He lifted her hand to his lips and touched her fingers to them. The contact was just as electric as it was brief. Her skin against his mouth grew warm. She wondered, could he feel the heat that his kiss

26

generated? For just a moment, Brendan's eyes met hers and held them.

"Of course" was all she said.

He smiled and was gone, accompanied by Marge Kent. She introduced him to a woman whom Lisa recognized as the managing editor of the magazine. Lisa watched as the woman's eyes lit up and her smile grew wider. Brendan Donovan managed that effect on all women, it seemed, including Lisa.

Steve was ordering another round of drinks. His agent had moved on to a neighboring table.

"Quite the charmer, our Mr. Donovan." Steve's voice betrayed more than a touch of jealousy, and Lisa noticed with alarm that he was beginning to slur his words.

Lisa refrained from reminding Steve that he, too, had a reputation as a ladies' man. Instead she said icily, "Business all wrapped up with Freddy?"

He took her point and dropped his eyes. "You're right to be angry, Lisa. But I didn't intend for Freddy to monopolize my time. This is *our* night, from now on."

As he spoke, Lisa saw one of the girls who had been sitting with Freddy—the Racquel Welch look-alike—approach them.

"Steve," the girl said in honeyed tones, "Freddy says we're checking out here. Meet us at Skipper's on the West Side later? Freddy said he wants you to meet Mr. Goldsmith."

Steve mumbled his reply. It was somewhere between a yes and a no. To Lisa he said, "Mr. Goldsmith is the financial genius I was telling you about. He advised—"

"—Reggie Jackson and a slew of other baseball players about keeping Uncle Sam from gobbling up all their money," Lisa finished for him. She was silent for a moment.

"Steve," she said finally, "perhaps this just isn't meant to be our evening. To tell you the truth, I'm planning to

27

leave here after I get a minute to talk with Marge. You go with Freddy and the . . . gang. I'll take a taxi home."

"That's nonsense, Lisa. What kind of guy do you think—"

"I won't think any less of you, Steve. *Promise.* We'll get together when I get back in town, okay? Then we'll *really* talk."

She needed breathing room. Time to think. To be alone. She was not ready for an emotional scene later tonight with Steve.

"You're sure?" Steve's brawny, callused hands were on her shoulders.

Lisa nodded. "Good night, Steve. I'll call you." On tiptoe, she brushed her lips against his cheek. Then she turned and walked over to the *Lifestyle* staffers who had gathered in front of the bar. A last glance confirmed her expectations. Steve, Freddy, and two girls were making their way to the exit.

Marge was at her side in an instant. The older woman wore a sympathetic expression. She was like a favorite aunt to Lisa because Marge was the kind of person who, although interested in your moves, didn't attempt to choreograph them for you.

"You could have knocked me over with a feather!" Marge exclaimed loud enough for half a dozen people nearby to hear. "You with Steve again? I never . . ."

"Never say never," Lisa warned her with a laugh.

"Touché." Marge grinned. She had never married and Lisa thought that it was probably because of her devotion to her career. Few men could have compared to the excitement and challenge Marge Kent found in her job at *Lifestyle.* And still fewer would have understood the hours Marge put in striving to give the magazine her personal stamp of excellence, Lisa reflected.

"Didn't I promise you would be interested in the guest list?" Marge asked her. "I thought you would like to meet the World's Most Eligible Bachelor in advance of your first interview."

Lisa could think of dozens more dignified, professional ways in which to meet one's interview subject than on a dance floor, and she told Marge as much.

"How do I gain his trust if he thinks of me as someone who's a social butterfly, a disco gadabout?" Lisa asked with a trace of annoyance.

"I assure you, Lisa, he thinks nothing of the kind. As a matter of fact, he told me—"

"Marge, guess who's here?" Someone grabbed the editor's hand and propelled her toward another table.

Lisa failed to learn what, in fact, Brendan Donovan thought about her. It was probably just as well, she decided. She tried to erase the thought of him from her mind, and failed.

She became increasingly aware of the noise that surrounded her—the babble of voices, the throbbing beat of high-decibel music. Smoke swirled in the stuffy room, threatening to suffocate her if she didn't move.

Lisa needed fresh air to clear her head. The closest to outdoors was the rooftop. She made her way to the elevator and pressed the top button. In seconds, steel doors opened soundlessly to admit her. She stepped inside, her heels clicking on the polished floor. Inside, alone, she leaned her head on the cool, slick mirrored glass that lined the elevator. She felt as if she were in a futuristic cocoon, safe for the moment from the pressures of the outside world.

No sooner had she closed her eyes than the bell made a soft dinging sound at the sixtieth floor. The doors opened, and a few steps later she was walking out onto the rooftop garden. One shadowy couple shared the night, but they were oblivious to her presence.

Oh, to be in love again. Lisa quickly shrugged off the thought and walked over to the brick wall that lined the

29

edge of the rooftop garden. In a planter on the ledge, a row of hardy crimson-colored mums withstood the high-altitude winds of the city. She brushed her fingers along the feathery tops, and thought of nature's little miracle that allowed flowers like these to bloom again after last year's harsh, cold winter.

She shivered as the wind whipped around the corner and the mums bent under its force, temporarily mastered by nature's whim. Just as she had been momentarily mastered by the force of Brendan Donovan. The passage of a few minutes had not dimmed the memory of his hands about her waist, or his lips searing the flesh of her fingers.

She pinched her arms lightly. She would have to forget all that, the sooner the better. She had been contracted to write an article for *Lifestyle,* not to entertain romantic fantasies about its subject. Marge Kent would question her faith in Lisa if she knew what she was feeling right now.

Lisa took a few steps and rested her hands on the wrought-iron railing. She was glad she had decided to come up here before heading home. The couple had gone, and she was alone. On the roof, the noise of the city seemed a thousand miles away. Instead, the stars above her seemed close enough to catch. Lisa thought that if she stretched, she might touch the nearest star, it seemed so near.

The well-known children's poem came back to her and she softly whispered the words:

"Star light, star bright, first star I've seen to-night . . ."

A deep masculine voice from behind her finished, ". . . I wish I may, I wish I might, have the wish I wish tonight."

Startled, Lisa turned to look into Brendan Donovan's eyes.

"You still do that too?" she asked him.

He nodded, and an easy smile touched his features. "I wished on so many stars when I was a kid, I almost ran out of them."

A soft glow from the garden's gas lanterns reflected Brendan's silhouette. Lisa said nothing for the moment, letting her gaze rest on him. What she saw was a man who seemed taller than the six feet stated in his biography. His tapered body was the kind that clothiers loved; lean yet well-muscled, it held a masculine gracefulness that was inborn, never acquired. The expertly tailored black-on-black tuxedo that he wore accentuated the impact. What had she thought of him while looking at the newspaper clippings . . . uncharacteristic looks? That much was true, she reflected. His face just missed handsomeness. Perhaps it was the leanness of his features or the iron set of the jaw, broken only when he was smiling. As he was now.

"But surely," Lisa said at last, "most of your wishes came true?"

Brendan advanced a few steps until he was beside her. Next to him, her forehead came just below his chin. She was suddenly uncomfortable from the nearness of him. *Calm down,* she told herself. *This isn't the time to be impressed by celebrity . . . again.*

Brendan answered her. "Eventually *some* of my wishes came true." Then he laughed, self-mockingly. "Thank God, not everything. I might have been in real trouble."

Lisa nodded her head. "What's the saying? 'Be careful what you ask for . . . you might get it'?"

"Exactly. And you? Are you a frequent stargazer? Daily visitor to wishing wells? Have you invested a fortune in pennies tossed in fountains?" He was looking down at her, a half-grin cracking those granite features.

She giggled softly. "I was always wishing I could *stop* wishing, so I could begin to collect coins for my piggy bank. Never managed to, though."

31

"But an admirable endeavor, saving," Brendan said, "especially for a woman like you."

Lisa puzzled over that remark, but before she could question him he had taken her hand and pulled it up over their heads along with his hand, directing her gaze to one particularly bright star.

He said, "Go ahead . . . make a wish. I'll make one too. And when they both come true someday, we'll tell each other about them."

Silently she did as he suggested. His hand held hers at his side then, as if it were the most natural thing in the world. Lisa gazed at the curtain of night above them, then out toward the city below them. Manhattan shimmered in the night as a thousand lights glowed, some swiftly moving, others quite still. The World Trade Center rose in the distance. She could just make out the building that housed the *Lifestyle* offices.

Did wishing on the same star with one's interview subject constitute a compromise of journalistic principles? Lisa chuckled briefly at the thought, not sure if her sudden giddiness was the result of the unaccustomed altitude, the gin in the gin and tonics finally catching up with her, or the intoxicating nearness of Brendan Donovan.

"Sshh. You'll break the spell, love."

Lisa looked up through thick dark lashes to find his gaze just inches from her own. The world stopped then, and she forgot all about wishing upon stars. Suddenly she was wishing desperately for him to kiss her. Never mind that they hardly knew each other, that she was a reporter assigned to write about him. There was only here and now.

And then his lips found hers. Beneath his gently probing kiss, her lips responded. Her arms found their way up his shoulders as his hands tightened on the small of her back and he pressed her body, gently yet insistently, toward his. The clinging fabric of her dress seemed suddenly no more significant than a flimsy nightgown as once again she burned exquisitely beneath his touch.

She had never been kissed as Brendan Donovan kissed her. She trembled as the sharp thrust of his tongue parted her lips and found the hidden recesses that she herself had never known were there. His fingers caressed her shoulders, then her bare nape, sending delicious shivers down the length of her body.

The more he kissed her, the more she wanted him to. The longer they stood pressed together against the chill of night, the longer she knew that here was a man like no other she had ever known.

It was not a predatory kiss, not at all. Rather, Brendan's mouth claimed hers in a deliberate exploration, as if he meant to take all the time in the world discovering her secrets. She felt the strength and stiffness drain from her body, and in their place felt liquid and warmth. If he could provoke such a response from her with a kiss, imagine . . . no, the thought was better left unimagined.

"Brendan . . ." she whispered, and as his name escaped her raw, thoroughly kissed lips, she came to her senses. What was she thinking of, kissing him?

She disengaged herself from his embrace; he did not fight her, just as his kiss had not meant to thoroughly possess her. Again, Lisa had the maddening feeling that he was merely biding his time, content to wait for the opportune moment.

Lisa slowly backed away from him until she was at a safe distance of two feet. It was not enough to prevent a last-minute longing to rush right back into his arms. She fought to control her trembling, and straightened her shoulders. Brendan was staring at her with an expression that was impossible to read by the light of the flickering lamps.

She faltered. "I . . . we won't let this happen again,

33

will we?" Her voice sounded strained, unlike her. "I mean . . ." She took a deep breath. "That's not exactly the behavior Marge Kent has a right to expect from her reporter. I . . . didn't expect it myself."

"Really?" Brendan's thick, straight eyebrows rose half an inch, and his eyes probed hers. "I wanted to kiss you from the time I asked you to dance. I couldn't find the appropriate moment . . . until now."

"Yes . . . well." She bit her lower lip, not trusting herself to meet his gaze. "Now that we've satisfied our curiosity about each other, perhaps we can get down to business the next time we meet. And I'll be able to do what I've been hired to do."

The muscles in his jaw tensed. She wished she could read his thoughts.

He shrugged. "Sorry to put such a damper on things. I rather thought it was a pleasant introduction. You, er, responded similarly."

Lisa groped for a quick comeback. "It's not that," she said. "You must remember, it's not every day that I'm kissed by a famous race car driver."

Brendan didn't smile. Instead he said, with an unfamiliar twist of the mouth that had just caressed hers, "Nor have I, by an up-and-coming investigative reporter who is also a social butterfly."

Now it was Lisa's turn to be surprised. "One party at Roulette makes me a social butterfly?" she asked incredulously.

"No, but certainly the company you keep tells me that you're not a stranger to New York night life."

"The company I keep . . ." Lisa repeated, the implications of the remark sinking in. "Steve Hanley?"

She tore her eyes away from Brendan's and studied the Manhattan lights spread out beneath them, searching for the right answer. She decided she did not owe Brendan

Donovan an account of her love life, or rather her *former* love life.

"He happens to be an old friend," she informed Brendan finally, looking him in the eyes once again. "And how I spend my evenings, and with whom, has no bearing on my job as a journalist, Mr. Donovan." She smiled tightly as she said the last. "If you feel less threatened by the thought of me as a 'social butterfly,' be my guest."

He regarded her silently. Then, "It's not I who feels threatened, Miss Taylor. One of us can't seem to make up her mind tonight."

Lisa clasped her hands together tightly to steady herself. "I've already made up mine, thank you. Shall we call it a night?"

Standing beside him in the elevator that would descend to Roulette, Lisa focused on the row of shiny black buttons that designated each floor. The silence, which had seemed soothing on the way up to the rooftop, now hung over them like a spider's web, trapping her in its suffocating embrace.

For his part, Brendan didn't seem to mind the quiet. He stood straight and oddly tense, drumming his perfectly manicured fingers on the railing that ran around the elevator's interior. Once he glanced at his gold watch as if he could not part with his present companion a moment too soon.

The doors opened with cool precision and Lisa felt as if she dared breathe again. Brendan stopped and fixed his gaze on her.

"A rather awkward beginning . . . or a very auspicious one, depending on how you look at it, Miss Taylor. I'll see you at Hilton Head?"

Lisa nodded with what seemed a major effort. Her head felt like it was made of lead, it hung so heavily on her neck.

"Of course," she told him.

36

CHAPTER THREE

The Roulette doorman signaled for a taxi. When it screeched to a stop, Lisa sank gratefully into the backseat and hung on to the armrest as the driver, in the no-holds-barred tradition of New York City hacks, scooted off with horn blaring. She gave the driver her address in Greenwich Village.

Lisa felt numb, her brain like a master computer that had been overloaded. Now, she reflected, instead of arriving at Brendan Donovan's home on Hilton Head Island as an unbiased journalist, she would arrive as the woman whom Mr. Eligible had last kissed. Correction, Lisa told herself. By next week, such a ladies' man was bound to have made another conquest or two. She would be one of *many* whom he had kissed.

She closed her eyes and rested her head on the back of the seat. She willed herself to think positive thoughts. The Maish Lawrence article *had* been one of her best and its publication would surely advance her career. If she kept her mind on her job, her nose to the grindstone, herself away from Brendan Donovan's electrifying touch, the Donovan piece could be another winner.

At the very least, she would benefit from a visit to the glorious island. Although there were numerous hotels and condominiums available, Brendan had insisted that the magazine's reporter must stay at his home. He explained that he kept odd hours, that he often flew his twin-engine plane to distant parts at a moment's notice, and that he couldn't be bothered making appointments with a reporter who did not offer immediate accessibility.

Lifestyle had agreed to the ground rules. The magazine, anxious for Lisa to cover her subject thoroughly, had promised that its reporter would keep a low profile during the celebrity's trips.

Low profile, thought Lisa. After tonight she felt like keeping the lowest possible profile—would digging a hole in the ground and crawling into it achieve that aim? What must Brendan think of a reporter who had so conveniently misplaced her professionalism just in time to be kissed?

Lisa opened her eyes. It was no use. She would just have to live with the incident and try to overcome any ill effects.

The taxi jerked to a stop in front of her apartment in the fashionable brownstone. Quickly she pulled a five-dollar bill from her purse and paid the driver. At her door, she fumbled for her keys.

Anxiety stiffened her fingers, so that unlocking the door became a complicated task. It was an unfortunate habit of hers, she knew; whenever she became nervous, parts of her normally cooperative body refused to listen to the signals transmitted by her brain. Safely inside her apartment, she flicked on the nearest table lamp.

Lisa kicked off her shoes and carried them into the bedroom after first turning off the lamp. In her bedroom, by the faint glow emanating from her clock radio, she quickly stripped off her dress, half-slip, and stockings, unsnapping her lacy bra and letting it drop to the floor.

She entered the bathroom, where she quickly rinsed her face of its makeup and brushed her hair the requisite one hundred strokes. Then she slipped between the cool white sheets of her bed. Tomorrow she would dutifully give herself a facial and pick up her clothes and even do

38

her laundry. Tonight she craved restful sleep. As she drifted off, she told herself that she wished the evening's events with Brendan had never occurred. Yet, another voice in the night whispered that she was glad.

Lisa's slim hands gripped the steering wheel. *Not now,* she prayed silently, *not here.* A strange hissing noise was coming from under the hood of the car. That didn't worry her as much as the steam, which rolled out along with the hissing sound.

She was on the freeway, just outside of Florence, South Carolina, on her way to Hilton Head Island. It was early afternoon on the second day of her journey.

The car was a rental, from an agency she had dealt with before. But here she was, blessed with a hissing, smoking Chevy that showed signs of abandoning her. An exit sign loomed up ahead and she gratefully acknowledged the FOOD and GAS signs alongside it.

She eased up on the gas pedal as the car began its descent down the ramp. *If it's something minor,* she thought, *I'll still have plenty of time to make it to Brendan's before dark.* Cautiously she steered the little compact into the first service station she spied.

An attendant ambled over. As he drew closer, she saw that the name CORKY was stenciled on his navy blue work shirt. He was shaking his head in sympathy.

"You sound like you got problems, lady. Wanna pull your hood latch and I'll have a look-see?"

She found the latch under the dashboard and gave it a swift pull. The hood popped reluctantly, as if unwilling to be examined, fixed, and thus returned to the rigors of the road.

The attendant, a red-haired young man Lisa guessed at high school age, leaned over the engine and disappeared from her view.

Lisa opened her door and got out to stretch her legs.

She walked toward the front of the car and made a pretense of examining the engine along with Corky. She didn't know a piston from an alternator. The engine could have been missing its radiator, carburetor, and battery for all she knew about cars, but she wasn't about to let the attendant in on that fact. It would only further the stereotypical thinking about women and cars, Lisa reasoned. Besides, someday she really intended to educate herself about the mechanization of an automobile. Someday.

"Right here's your problem, ma'am." The attendant pointed a greasy finger at the offending part. "Radiator hose, just like I thought. It's plumb cracked."

"Oh," Lisa said. "I imagine you'll have to patch it . . . or something?"

Corky laughed. "No, ma'am. You'll need a brand-new one." Lisa resigned herself to the delay and made herself comfortable—if that was the right word—on the plastic-covered seat in the cluttered office.

Three hours later, Lisa folded the magazines she had been reading into her soft leather briefcase and strolled over to the service bay. Corky had just slammed the hood of her car.

"All set, ma'am. Sorry it took so long . . . we had to search the whole county for your radiator hose. Lemme figure up your bill." While he totaled the costs, Lisa dug out Brendan's telephone number for the third time. She let the telephone ring ten times, with no answer, before she replaced the receiver in its cradle. She would try again on down the road.

Fifteen dollars and thirty-seven cents poorer, she was on her way once again. She was regretting her decision to drive to South Carolina rather than book a flight, as was the customary procedure. True, it had been just the scenic drive she had looked forward to, with stops here and there at quaint country shops and roadside inns with menus featuring hominy grits, but she worried now about the delay. Brendan Donovan had expected his guest to be there by now. She suspected he was a man who didn't appreciate being kept waiting.

An hour later she stopped to put in another call to Brendan. An older man's voice answered on the second ring. Lisa asked for Brendan, but was told in rather gruff tones that he was unavailable.

"Could you please give him a message, then?" Lisa asked. She gave her name and said, "I've been trying to reach Mr. Donovan for several hours now to let him know I've had unexpected car trouble, but the car has been repaired and I'm on my way. I should be there by ten P.M. Please tell Mr. Donovan I am very sorry if this causes any inconvenience."

"I'll tell him, Miss Taylor. See you, now." He hung up, and Lisa was left listening to the dial tone.

Maybe, Lisa hoped, the man who possessed that voice was not as gruff as he sounded. Maybe.

A few hours later she drove over the bridged roadway that connected Hilton Head Island to mainland South Carolina. It was dark, so she could see little of her surroundings other than brief glimpses of trees caught in the glare of the Chevy's headlights.

On the seat beside her Lisa spread out a map of the island. A red circle indicated the location of Brendan's home. Lisa shone her pen-sized flashlight on the map as she drove slowly along the winding, tree-lined road.

At a guardhouse, she gave her name and Brendan's. The guard checked against a typed list on his bulletin board and gave her a pass, admitting her to the island's residential area.

Seven miles later she turned right at a sign marked PRIVATE. The address matched the one penciled in on her map. She drove cautiously and soon reached the end of the long gravel drive. She was not fully prepared for the sight that lay in silhouette before her.

A sprawling contemporary home of cedar, stone, and glass was spotlighted dramatically in its heavily treed setting. Lisa guessed that it was at least five times as large as her aunt and uncle's home and *that* had seemed abundantly spacious to her as a child. She was about to take a peek at a different lifestyle, she guessed, one in which opulence was right at home.

Lisa parked her car in a little side-lot alongside a tan four-wheel-drive vehicle. The engine settled as she turned the key. As she got out of the car, she heard the night sounds of the island, along with a dog's bark, muffled as if the animal was being restrained inside the house.

More lights burst the darkness of the night as the massive front doors opened. She saw Brendan standing in the stark light of the porch lamp. He walked over to her car, where she began busily retrieving her luggage from the trunk.

"I was beginning to doubt you were planning to arrive this evening," he said, frowning at her. He took the two heaviest suitcases and handed her the lightest one. "Car trouble, you said? Or do you treat all of your appointments so lightly?"

"Not at all. It was a cracked radiator hose," she informed him, trying her best to indicate her vast knowledge of engine parts. "It's all fixed now."

Brendan's eyebrows rose. In disbelief? Lisa wondered. He was saying, with more than a touch of sarcasm, "Those radiator hose problems *are* bearish . . . *very* complicated. Takes hours to fix them."

He was mocking her.

Lisa thought, *Let him have his little entertainment at my expense. I'll not dignify his rudeness with an explanation.* As if she had delayed her arrival on purpose!

He asked her about the trip then. Had the roads been

42

good? No detours? Hotel room adequate? Map to his house readable? Lisa answered, in a friendly, conversational tone that belied the churning in the pit of her stomach.

It was difficult to believe that here was the man who had kissed her so passionately only days earlier. If he was reminded of it—or if he even remembered it—he gave no sign. Lisa decided that the best course of action for her was to adopt a similar attitude. She reminded herself silently that such nonchalance was what she wanted. Her integrity as a journalist depended on burying that little episode.

Brendan unloaded her luggage on the slate floor of the foyer. "Your home away from home, Miss Taylor." His large, competent-looking hands swept out to indicate the interior of his home.

"It's beautiful," Lisa told him sincerely, for it was the most stunning home she had ever been in. Not that it was ostentatious or overbearing or even particularly rich-looking. No, its power lay in its simplicity.

Forest-green carpet spread out over the lush expanse of a Great Room. Light oak contemporary furniture, upholstered in creamy white Haitian cotton, was grouped in an eminently comfortable arrangement around a massive natural-stone fireplace. The chimney rose to the top of the vaulted cathedral ceiling. On each side, bookcases were filled to overflowing with well-thumbed volumes. Lisa caught a glimpse of several popular best sellers along with classic works by Dickens and Mark Twain. An old-fashioned ceiling fan, Lisa noticed, would create a welcome stir of air in the hot days of summer.

She took in the dozen or so leafy green plants in the room. Someone had a green thumb, aided by the natural sunlight that surely filtered through the full-length glass windows on the far side of the room.

Lisa could see little outside those windows but a

murky blackness that hovered beyond a wooden deck. She heard the faint yet insistent crashing noise in close proximity that she recognized as the ocean meeting the shoreline of the island.

She turned to Brendan and smiled. "How do you ever manage to leave this place? It's heaven."

Brendan's mouth quirked in amusement as he picked up her luggage once again. "Heaven, perhaps . . . but not especially exciting if a person is inclined to do a little hell-raising," he told her.

Of course, Lisa thought. She had momentarily forgotten his reputation.

She followed him down a long, grass-colored hallway. He indicated the ceiling above her with a nod of his head. "Russ lives upstairs in this wing. He's the fellow you talked to on the phone. . . ."

Talked to, Lisa thought, was stretching the truth.

". . . You'll meet him tomorrow, along with Flannagan . . . that's the dog you heard when you pulled up. He's a devil, that one, but a charming rogue all the same. You do like dogs?"

Lisa shook her head. "Sorry, I've always been partial to cats." At least, she thought privately, cats don't bark as if they intend to bite your head off.

"Cats are a bit too devious for my liking," Brendan said. "You never know where you stand with them." Why did Lisa feel as if she had just been put in the same category?

"Here's your room," Brendan said. He led her into a spacious bedroom, tastefully furnished in natural wicker with peach accents and silk-covered walls. A huge bed filled the center of the room, looking comfortable and inviting with a satin comforter folded at its foot. A walk-in closet and well-lighted dressing area completed the picture. The door to a well-stocked bathroom stood partially ajar.

44

The entire house, Lisa realized, was perhaps a reflection of the real Brendan Donovan. Although his public image was racy, hard-driving, and a bit on the wild side, his home was a peaceful sanctuary. What she saw was a restful, comfortable environment that hinted at solitary evenings spent reading by the fire. Perhaps there were two sides to Brendan's personality. Perhaps her task was to match the colors of his personal Rubik's Cube and thus solve the puzzle of his enigmatic personality. She meant to find out.

"You'll be comfortable here?" Brendan interrupted her reverie.

"Yes, very. Thank you," Lisa said. In the soft light of the bedroom's wicker fan-lamps, she studied Brendan's face. Was she imagining it, or had the hard lines etched around his mouth softened just a bit in the few minutes since her arrival? Outside New York City he seemed relaxed, at ease, less the dynamic jetsetter and more the contented beach bum.

She dared to meet his glance. His brown eyes gazed steadily at hers in return, and his brows lifted in a quizzical expression. At last he said, "A man's home is his castle. Now, I would guess, you're attempting to define me for your article based on what you see here. Correct?"

Lisa blushed. He had an uncanny knack for reading her thoughts. A very perceptive man, Brendan Donovan.

"You're only partially correct, Brendan . . . er, Mr. Donovan," Lisa said. "I was also thinking about the phrase having to do with 'a house divided.' "

Again he gave her that quizzical look.

"I'm sure you'll explain that one to me in due time," he said, moving swiftly around her to open the heavy curtains that covered the entire length of one wall. He flicked a switch as he drew the curtains.

Lisa gasped. Under white floodlights, not twenty feet from her sliding-glass door, was an olympic-size swimming pool. It was irregularly shaped to accommodate the jutting angles of the wooden deck off the Great Room. A cedar hot tub stood on the edge of the deck, wrapped in privacy by scrub oak trees.

"Since you won't be interviewing me or writing *all* the time you're here, I suggest you get some use out of the pool. It's great exercise," Brendan told her.

Lisa strode across the room to stand beside him, staring out at the still blue water, dormant in the night with not a ripple on its smooth surface.

"Wonderful," said Lisa, and she meant it. Her bathing suit would be put to good use as soon as she had the chance. "Thank you for . . . for making me feel so welcome," she said.

Brendan winked slowly at her. "Pools I can provide, m'lady." He pointed toward the black sky, just visible through the trees. No light penetrated the thick curtain of clouds. "But we'll have to wait another night to carry on our conversation with the stars. If, that is, you can squeeze it in among all your journalistic endeavors."

Lisa ignored the slight sarcasm in his voice and the reference to her rather awkward ending of their rooftop kiss that now seemed ages ago.

"I might manage, at that," she said sweetly.

Brendan was striding toward her door. "I'll leave you to unpack and settle in tonight . . . the kitchen's on the other side of the Great Room, if you need anything. We start the day early here . . . Russ makes a terrific breakfast. *Promptly* at eight o'clock."

Lisa gulped, trying to hide her dismay. She was a night person; she could barely open her eyes by nine. Talking was impossible until ten or so. Putting food into her mouth was accomplished shortly after noon. *You'll adjust,* she told herself. *You have to.*

". . . And Lisa," Brendan was saying, "you can cut out the 'Mr. Donovan' business. I think our relationship

46

has . . . ah . . . moved beyond the introductory stage, wouldn't you agree?" He said this with a perfectly straight face, but his brown eyes were twinkling. "Good night." He shut the door soundlessly behind him.

Lisa had to laugh. Brendan had certainly lost none of his charm since their first meeting at Roulette.

She lifted her suitcases and rested them on the bed to unpack. In short order she had her traveling wardrobe, such as it was, tucked away in drawers and the ample closet. Next she treated herself to a scented bath. The fragrance of wild flowers lulled her to a relaxation that bordered on dozing, as she luxuriated in the large, peach-tinted sunken tub.

The mirrors that surrounded the tub on three sides offered the chance for a frank appraisal. Damp blond tendrils escaped the hasty bundle atop her head. A long graceful neck extended from shoulders that Aunt Phyllis called "too wide to be demure, my dear, but perfect for today's ridiculous designer fashions." Lisa thought that they suited her just fine. High, full breasts accentuated her womanliness; her waist and hips were blessedly narrow, her legs unexpectedly long for her five feet six.

She soaped herself leisurely and came to the realization that everything, bathing included, moved at a leisurely pace here. Compared to the frenetic hurrying that was as much a part of New York City life as crowds and street vendors, island life might as well have taken place on another planet.

Lisa decided she would appreciate the slowed pace while she could.

She squeezed the thick washcloth over her breasts, enjoying the delicious surge of water that trickled onto her flat stomach. She closed her eyes and, unbidden, Brendan's face etched itself in her mind. Then it seemed as if the hands washing her body were not her hands at all anymore, but Brendan's. They were large and strong and knowing, and they moved over her nakedness with instinctively sure strokes.

Was this what Brendan's lovemaking would feel like? Was he gentle and strong at the same time, achingly tender and roughly passionate in the same breath? Two sides, Lisa thought, remember the man can be the opposite of what he seems.

Lisa'a hand on the washcloth doubled into a fist. Why did she permit herself such a fantasy, when her interest in Brendan must be confined to discovering his personality and writing about it? She would do well to forget the lean, hard-muscled lines of his body and the eyes that burned straight into her soul. She was here to capture him for *Lifestyle*'s pages, not for her own romantic fantasies. And she shouldn't forget, she reminded herself, that a significant aspect of that personality had to do with his womanizing.

She shivered with a sudden chill and quickly stepped out of the bathtub, toweling herself vigorously. Her skin's pink tone heightened.

She walked into the bedroom to the closet and slipped on a sheer nylon nightgown, loosening her long hair as she did so. Turning off all the lamps except one, she climbed into the massive bed, sliding down between smooth silk sheets. She set her portable alarm for 7:30 A.M. She would become a morning person if it killed her —which it probably would.

Determined to take her mind off Brendan, Lisa opened one of several books she had packed. Perry Mason mysteries were a passion of hers, and she delved into the first chapter of this one. By page 29 she was nodding off to sleep. A drowsy thought came to her. Perhaps the island's ambience was changing her, too. When was the last time she'd fallen asleep before midnight?

Rrrrring! Lisa's left hand shot out from under her pillow to silence the insistent noise of the alarm. She pried open her blue eyes enough to see the hands on the clock. She had exactly half an hour until breakfast. Swiftly she sat up and finger-brushed her hair from her eyes, then went into the bathroom, where she splashed ice-cold water on her face.

Lisa risked a look in the mirror at her slightly puffy eyes, but other than that she looked almost human. She made a face at herself and laughed. That was more like it.

She followed the same routine she adhered to at home. Fifteen minutes of exercise—stretching muscles, touching toes, sit-ups and the like—got her blood circulating. With deft fingers she quickly set her long hair in electric rollers, took a brief shower, then carefully applied a minimum of makeup. Her hair took two minutes to brush and style. There! She felt ready to face Brendan and Russ and the mysterious canine Flannagan, wherever the latter was lurking this morning.

She slipped on a pair of jet-black denims, low-slung sandals, and a dolman-sleeved white top that hung loosely from her shoulders and gathered at the waist.

She found the kitchen, led by the sound of a whirring blender. It was, as Brendan had said, on the other side of the Great Room. She caught her first sight of Russ *and* Flannagan over the pair of swinging wooden doors that led from the hall into the kitchen.

Russ was busy cracking fresh white eggs into a glass bowl. He turned to face Lisa when he heard her footsteps.

He had the kind of face, Lisa thought, that exactly matched the voice she had heard on the phone yesterday. Rough, weathered, impatient to get on with things. Fine lines traced their way from the corners of his eyes to clipped silver hair, thinning on top. Lisa guessed his age to be sixtyish. But his wiry frame, clothed in a freshly

49

pressed pair of blue overalls over a colorfully checkered work shirt, belied his age. He had the look of a younger man, the result, Lisa guessed, of his outdoor-oriented life.

Flannagan, a huge Irish setter whose beautiful red head came close to Russ's waist, was watching the break-fast-preparation proceedings with great interest. The dog sensed Lisa's presence and came trotting over to inspect the new arrival. Lisa pushed open the swinging doors.

"Good morning. You're Russ, I take it?"

Russ turned at the sound of her voice. "I am. And you must be Lisa Taylor. Brendan said you'd be along about now."

His voice was low and gravelly, as if he had spent too many years shouting over the noise of car engines in order to be heard. Lisa knew he was a former race car mechanic and had, in fact, introduced Brendan to the sport.

Russ nodded toward the setter. "That's Flannagan, in case Brendan didn't introduce him last night." The dog began to circle Lisa warily, sniffing at the air around her, as if it would indicate whether she was friend or foe.

"Careful, now," Russ warned as she crouched with her hand outstretched, palm upward, toward Flannagan. No time like the present to start changing her attitude toward the species.

"He doesn't take well to strangers. A one-man dog, Brendan says, and I guess he's right. Well, lookee there."

Flannagan had ventured far enough to sniff Lisa's palm with his cold black nose. His whiskers brushed her skin, tickling her. And then he licked her hand with his great pink tongue in one encompassing swoop.

"Do I pass inspection, Flannagan, huh?" Lisa chuck-led, petting the dog's silky red-maned neck. Perhaps she might actually like him, after all. A one-man dog, was he? Maybe he just wasn't used to a woman's touch.

50

She looked up at Russ, who had busied himself at the counter once again. "Can I help with anything?"

"All taken care of," he assured her. "Like scrambled eggs? Raspberry jam? Fresh-squeezed orange juice . . . whole wheat toast?"

She nodded happily. "Will Brendan be joining us?"

She had heard no sounds of his stirring yet this morning.

"No, ma'am. He went into town on some errands. Said to tell you he's sorry not to get started with your interviews right away, but it couldn't be helped. So we'll just enjoy this breakfast together."

"When will he be back?" Lisa tried to dismiss the annoyance that tugged at her. Brendan was the interview subject, after all, and he was calling the shots for now.

"Didn't say," Russ answered. "But I 'spect it'll be sometime around noon."

Noon! Lisa wondered what she was supposed to do until then. Twiddle her thumbs? Play catch with Flannagan? She frowned. If Brendan regarded her job—her schedule—in such a cavalier manner, how cooperative and self-revealing was he going to be for the article? She sighed. Then it occurred to her that maybe Brendan's absence was a blessing in disguise. Here was a perfect opportunity to talk to Russ, without the somewhat intimidating presence of Brendan to possibly influence his remarks. It could be a productive morning after all.

Russ was saying, "Brendan mentioned you might want to use the pool. It's downright nice out there, what with the sun ashinin'."

"Sounds wonderful," Lisa assured him. She planned to swim to her heart's content in a little while, *after* she had talked to Russ. She moved to the sink to wash her hands of Flannagan's rather doggy smell.

"I got an apology to make," Russ told her offhandedly. "When you called yesterday to say you'd be late,

51

Brendan wasn't here and durn if I didn't forget to tell him. What reminded me was you gettin' here. By then it didn't make much difference."

"I guess that's why Brendan acted a bit put out when I finally did arrive," Lisa mused, more to herself than to Russ.

"Well, you just tell him that it weren't no fault of yours, miss."

Russ had breakfast ready to put on the table. He knocked on the table's wooden top. "Well, now that's settled, let's eat."

She settled on the cushion-covered seat of a spindle-backed Windsor chair. Flannagan claimed his—usual?—spot directly underneath the table. Russ set her food-laden breakfast plate on the natural-woven place mat in front of her and joined her across the table.

While they ate, Lisa quickly reviewed what she knew about her subject. Brendan's biography had already informed her that he had been an orphan and had been raised in a succession of foster homes until the age of fourteen, when he came to live with Russ. The older man, who worked as a mechanic on the southern race car circuit, had ignited Brendan's interest in cars and racing. Now she wanted to know more about his feelings, the real person who hid behind the charming mask of aloofness.

"Brendan has said in previous interviews that he was a 'wild kid' before you took him in," Lisa said. "What changed his ways? Was it love or discipline . . . or maybe both?"

Russ chuckled, a deep, rich sound that welled up in his thick chest and tumbled forth with hearty good cheer. "Nobody changed Brendan but *Brendan,*" he insisted. "He's a stubborn man and he was more so as a boy, if you can imagine."

52

"You introduced something into his life, obviously, that he could take an interest in?" Lisa prompted.

Russ nodded, considering the question. "That boy needed to have his energy—his natural orneriness, I called it—channeled into something positive. When he came to my house, I handed him a pair of overalls and a socket wrench and showed him how to use it."

"He was good with cars?"

Russ's eyes lit up at the memory. "He was a mechanical genius, that Brendan. 'Course, that was nothin' compared to what happened when he got behind a wheel. Nobody saw nothin' but dust after that!"

He laughed and began gathering up the breakfast dishes. "That reminds me, young lady, I could sit here jawin' with you all day, but I got chores to do myself." He rose from the table. "Ask me some more questions this evenin', if you've a mind."

Lisa thanked him. "Let me do the dishes," she suggested. If the way to this man's confidentiality was through his pots and pans, she was prepared to make a considerable domestic effort.

But he waved her off. "I just put 'em in the dishwasher," he told her. "My own special way, too. Don't nobody mess with the system but me."

Thus dismissed, Lisa returned to her room, mulling over Brendan's suggestion of a swim in the pool in his absence. She glanced out the glass doors at the sparkling water.

So Brendan had errands in town despite the fact that she had an editor to please and a deadline to meet. Would this be the pattern of their days together—Lisa anxious to pin him down for meaningful conversation, and Brendan just as anxious to elude her probing questions with convenient disappearing acts?

Lisa's mouth dried uncomfortably at the thought. Brendan Donovan could turn out to be one of those reti-

53

cent, impenetrable subjects—like Johnny Carson, say, or Marlon Brando—who refused to open up before the public eye.

Lisa envisioned the reaction at *Lifestyle* if she failed to come up with a winner on Brendan Donovan. A "kill fee," if she was lucky—a small sum for the time she had put in on an article that the editors subsequently deemed unsuitable. And after that? Article assignments would be more difficult to come by . . . if they came at all.

She squared her shoulders. Whatever Brendan had in mind, she had a goal also. This article would be her best to date, topping the Maish Lawrence piece, which Marge Kent had praised to the skies. This next one she would praise to the heavens, Lisa vowed. She smiled at the choice of words. She would need all the help she could get from heaven above on this one.

Lisa resolved to pin down Brendan the moment he walked into the house.

In the meantime, maybe she could score a few points in her favor by following his suggestion of a morning swim. But it would be the last time, she promised herself, that she followed his prescribed plan. She'd heard stories of "superstars" whose carefully orchestrated interview sessions were artfully arranged to reveal only what the subject wished to reveal. Usually these people employed a public relations person to manage this for them. Brendan, she reflected, needed no assistance; he was managing splendidly on his own.

She rummaged in the top drawer of the dresser for one of the bathing suits she had packed at the last minute. Now she was glad she had brought them. The temperature outside was getting warmer and maybe the pool would cool off her annoyance. She slipped on a kelly-green maillot and grabbed a brightly striped towel. Quickly, with practiced skill, she worked her long hair into a braid and wound it in a knot on top of her head, fastening the knot with a small silver clip.

Lisa slid the glass door along its track and stepped through the opening, closing the door behind her. She spotted a sturdy-looking blue canvas raft, already inflated, at the far end of the pool. She deposited her towel and book on a nearby chaise and skipped over to claim the raft.

Lisa carried it to the water's edge. Gingerly she dipped a pink-polished toe in the water. Brrrr! A nice leisurely float on the raft, she decided, had distinct advantages over a morning swim. Carefully she lowered the raft onto the pool's surface and eased herself onto it, stomach down.

Arms extended, she paddled slowly toward the center of the pool. She lay facedown, letting the sun warm her body. Her eyelids soon became heavy, and she thought drowsily that here was a perfect spot for a quick nap. She wasn't so accustomed to these early-bird hours after all.

CHAPTER FOUR

She floated, oblivious to everything except the gentle lapping of the water against the raft and the faraway sounds of the island birds. What an idyllic way to spend one's life . . . drifting atop blue, blue water . . .

A brief, almost indiscernible splashing sound broke the stillness. Lisa's eyes flew open as Brendan's head emerged from the water beside her. His dark, curly hair was plastered to his head, the tips glistening with droplets of crystal-clear water. The wetness only emphasized the strong, uncompromising lines of his face and the white, even teeth that he displayed now in a broad smile.

"A good way to spend the morning, isn't it?"

Lisa propped herself up silently on her elbows. Then she smiled sweetly to diffuse the reproach in her voice. "Only when you don't have an article deadline staring you in the face."

"Point taken." Brendan was treading water, his bronzed, well-muscled shoulders moving easily in a half circle just below the water's surface. With several deft moves he backstroked his way to the edge of the pool and hoisted himself up to sit on the ledge.

Lisa couldn't help noticing that his body had the hard, lean look she had suspected lurked underneath the well-cut clothes he usually wore. Like the cars he drove, he was sleek and perfectly proportioned. The brief black trunks he wore did little to diminish the fact of his pure maleness.

"By the way," Brendan said, "I took a look at your car engine this morning. It needs a thorough tune-up. Russ said he would be happy to do it."

"I would be grateful," Lisa acknowledged. "I'd be willing to pay him."

Brendan shook his head. "He wouldn't hear of it."

"Well . . ." Lisa countered, "maybe I'll take a turn in the kitchen as payment." She chuckled. "It'll certainly be easier on my budget that way. . . ."

Brendan looked disconcerted. The lines on his forehead deepened in puzzlement. "Funny, I never pictured you worrying about a budget."

"Why not?" Lisa asked. Now it was she who was puzzled.

"I was under the distinct impression that a woman like you, making the social scene with Steve Hanley and all that goes with it . . . that you didn't concern yourself with money."

Lisa couldn't believe what she was hearing. "Do you always make snap judgments about people before you get to know them?" She continued before he could interrupt, "You see me with Steve Hanley, and immediately you have me pegged as . . . as a sports groupie, or something." She was getting a full head of steam. "It's different when you're a man, isn't it? You can go dancing every damn night of the week, Mr. Brendan Donovan, and for all I know that's what you do, and I'm not to make any judgments based on that. But let me, a woman, socialize just a bit—*after* some long, hard weeks pounding at the typewriter, I might add—and I'm not serious about my work. Certainly not concerned about *money.*" Her voice dripped with sarcasm.

"Whoa, hold on a minute," Brendan said. "Let's not get into an argument over women's liberation and the right of the fairer sex to get out of the kitchen. I merely indicated that you didn't seem to be a woman who had to work for her money. You can blame that bit of misinformation on my friend who knew your uncle."

"Next time," Lisa suggested, "why don't you just concern yourself with preparing for an interview, not investigating the person who'll be interviewing you?"

"I'll consider it," Brendan said calmly. Was there a smile lurking behind the stone-faced facade?

Lisa couldn't let the matter drop just yet. "Please remember, I write because it's the best way I know to make a living . . . and I happen to be damn good at it," she added somewhat defiantly.

"Please accept my apologies, then." Brendan brushed back a strand of wet hair that had strayed onto his forehead. "Whew! That makes me out of line for the way I reacted last night when you arrived late," he continued. "I assumed . . . wrongly . . . that you were used to arriving at destinations whenever you pleased . . . a common failing among the jet-set ladies. . . . I don't usually greet guests with a frown."

"Apology accepted." Lisa smiled, and it reached far deeper than the outside of her face. That explained why Brendan had acted so displeased with her. And maybe, she reflected, it was why he had so casually gone off to town this morning and followed his schedule to the detriment of her own.

She looked up again to find him smiling at her. She chuckled softly. "I have a confession to make too. I assumed you went to town this morning in a deliberate move to play havoc with *my* schedule! I was going to grab you the minute you walked into the house and corner you with a million questions!"

"Why didn't you?"

"It's a bit difficult to pull that off while lazing about on a raft," she said, leaning on her right side while stroking the water from her comfortable perch. "It *is* awfully tempting to lie here and do nothing."

"Is it?" He grinned, slipping off the side of the pool and stroking toward her in a slow crawl. "You swim, I presume?"

"It's the one outdoorsy thing I do decently," she admitted.

"Good. I think it's about time you got some exercise!"

Before she knew what was happening, he dove beneath the surface, coming up beneath the raft and expertly flipping her over. She plunged into the chilly water, surprise registered by her mouth, open in protest. She came up sputtering and laughing.

She treaded water alongside him. The raft lay empty of its cargo, floating between them.

"And if I'd said I couldn't swim?" she gasped.

"Then you would've had the quickest lesson of your life!"

He was teasing, she knew. A man like Brendan pulled practical jokes only when he knew what the outcome would be.

"I hereby declare a truce!" His outstretched hand reached across the raft, ready to grasp hers. She extended her hand and allowed it to be enveloped in his. The touch sent a shiver down her spine. The water, she reminded herself, was extremely chilly. It was a wonder she hadn't shivered before now.

"And now, Miss L. B. Taylor, may I offer you the raft once again?" He pushed it toward her.

Lisa shook her head. "I think I've had enough for today." She shaded her eyes with her hand, glancing in the direction of the sun. "Maybe it's time we got down to business?"

She thought she detected a flicker of disappointment in his brown eyes. No, she decided, it was only the wavering

59

reflection from the pool, for he replied heartily, "That's what you're here for, isn't it? C'mon, I'll help you out."

Side by side they swam to the edge of the pool. Brendan hoisted himself easily to his feet and extended his hand. With one arm bracing against the ledge, she let him haul her out of the water. A ladder would have been so much more graceful, she reflected ruefully.

"Green is my favorite color," Brendan was saying. His eyes appraised her attire with an appreciative pause.

Lisa turned quickly away, aware that her cheeks were flushed. *Stop it,* she told herself. A compliment from a man like Brendan Donovan was like a . . . a passing comment about the day's weather from other men. *Remember Steve,* a voice inside her said.

She began toweling herself dry with the striped towel while Brendan did the same with his.

"We can get started on the interview whenever you like," Brendan said.

"How about right now?"

"Fine. We might as well enjoy the day . . . why don't we change into dry clothes and meet on the deck in, say, ten minutes?"

"Great." Lisa finished drying herself.

Inside, Lisa quickly slipped into a sundress and sandals. She unwound her wet hair from its confining braid and combed it out. She plugged in the cord to her hair dryer and gave a quick once-over to the wet strands. It would have to continue drying in the sun.

She checked herself in the mirror, noting the blush of color on her skin as it contrasted with the dusky colors of plum and peach on her flowered sundress. She pressed a spot on her shoulder with her forefinger. Definitely a hint of a sunburn. She'd better be careful, she thought, before she turned the shade of well-cooked lobster.

She gathered up her note pad, ball-point pen, a portable tape recorder, and a list of preliminary subject areas

60

and headed outside toward the deck. Brendan, dressed in drawstring shorts and a body-hugging navy blue T-shirt, was already there. He had drawn up two red canvas deck chairs to a glass-topped umbrella table. A pitcher, sweating with moisture and filled to the brim, was flanked by two tall, clear glasses.

Lisa settled herself in the chair on the left of Brendan. The umbrella offered welcome shade.

"Something cold to drink?" Brendan offered. Without waiting for an answer, he filled her glass. "I don't know whether you've tried this yet in New York. It's called Long Island iced tea, so maybe it's from your corner of the world. Anyway, it's just the thing for days like today."

He filled his own glass. "But I warn you . . . it's a fooler."

"Thanks for the warning." Lisa sipped cautiously at the icy concoction. It did taste deceptively like iced tea, but she suspected that its ingredients were far more potent.

"So . . . where do we start?" Brendan flashed a smile and Lisa was once again reminded of that same smile's prominence on magazine covers and tabloids around the world.

"Do we dive right in to the rumors of my supposed comeback in Formula One racing or shall we dissect my sordid past?" He was joking, of course, and yet Lisa thought she detected a glimmer of steel in the twinkling brown eyes, as if he was daring her to probe in either direction.

"First things first," Lisa replied. "You don't mind if I tape our conversation? It helps for accuracy."

"Go right ahead," Brendan assured her. "Although I must warn you I've been misquoted so many times, or had my words taken out of context, that I don't have much faith in the accuracy of the final outcome." He shrugged and continued in a philosophical tone, "You'll write what you want to write, tell readers what you want them to know." He arched his eyebrows at her mockingly. "Unless, of course, you're different from the hundred or so other journalists with whom I've come in contact."

Lisa sat up straighter in her chair. If he was deliberately baiting her, he was succeeding. She decided to play it cool.

"Have you considered that there are precious few reporters on St. Tropez, in Monaco, or Cannes, or Madrid, who would qualify for the Pulitzer prize? Come now, Mr. Donovan, writers who trail the jet set are, shall we say, a breed apart."

"Perhaps," he said noncommittally, regarding her coolly.

"Surely," she smiled, "you've come across several journalists who adhere to journalistic principles?"

"Maybe a few," he conceded.

"And perhaps they might, just might, hold different opinions of Brendan Donovan than he holds of himself, and so they write accordingly?"

"It's happened," he acknowledged with a smile. "But rarely. More often, I read things about me that are patently false or else are gross exaggerations."

"Is that why you agreed to this article? To try to clear up the misconceptions?" Lisa asked, her eyes intent on his expression, to store every detail in her memory. The time for scribbling notes would come later, in the privacy of her room.

"It's one of the reasons," Brendan agreed. "For instance, I've read that I was an instant success on the racing circuit. Nothing could be further from the truth, actually."

"Really? How was it, then?"

"I started racing when I was a kid, just eighteen or so.

And as Russ will verify, I had a hell of a lot to learn. The veterans were all too willing to demonstrate that fact to me." He grinned wryly at the memory. "I went through some pretty . . . enlightening, shall we say . . . times."

"Did you ever consider quitting? Getting started in a normal, nine-to-five career?"

"Never," Brendan stated firmly. "Frankly, I'm not sure I would fit too comfortably in the three-piece-suit world. I like to be my own boss . . . in charge, which I am behind the wheel of a car."

Lisa sipped her drink. Her gaze met his over the rim of her glass.

"But you've retired . . . or so you've stated publicly. Hasn't it been difficult to give up racing?"

He nodded, weighing his words carefully before he spoke, as if he was not quite sure how much he wanted to divulge.

"Very difficult. But necessary."

"In what way?" Lisa prompted.

He hesitated, as if wary of revealing too much of his inner self. "A race car driver," he said at last, "tempts fate every time he gets behind the wheel. The longer he races, the more risky his chances. Let's just say that I seemed to be playing a high-stakes game of chance . . . and it lost its charm for me."

Brendan flashed a grin, trying to diffuse his somber tone. But his eyes, Lisa saw, were deadly serious.

She knew she had to ask the next question. "The accident involving Guy Tremaine decided it for you?"

Brendan grimaced tightly. "Most definitely."

Lisa plunged ahead. "You and Guy were close friends before the accident. Have you been able to maintain that friendship since then?"

Brendan sipped at his drink, regarding her with a thoughtful expression. The brown eyes that had seemed so warm and inviting at poolside, now darkened to resemble the polished surface of charcoal. At last he said, "We still keep in touch. But, of course, it's different now that we're not competing."

"Does he harbor any bitterness, do you think?"

Brendan sighed, then gave a brief sort of half laugh, the kind a man gives when he's about to reveal much less than he is thinking.

"Bitterness is a debilitating disease, don't you think? And Guy told me he has enough physical problems—still —without adding another illness." Brendan took another stab at his drink, this time swallowing long and thirstily, as if to quench the memory of the fiery accident that had almost cost his friend's life.

Lisa phrased her next question carefully. She knew that Guy Tremaine was still being cared for in a private rehabilitation facility in Europe.

"Do you feel responsible for his injuries?"

Brendan returned her gaze with an unwavering stare. His answer, however, was anything but direct. "When I was racing, every time I got behind the wheel I knew that I held my life in my hands. I chose the profession, its thrills along with its potential disasters. What I was 'responsible' for, in those days, centered around my car, my pit crew, my corporate sponsor, and my abilities. It wasn't my job to maintain the track, or to sell tickets to spectators, or to test another driver's brakes."

He smiled slightly. "So you see, Lisa, asking me whether I feel responsible for Guy's injuries is asking an impossible question. Now, suppose you turn off that recorder and we'll turn to another subject. How good are your legs?"

Lisa stuttered in surprise. "H-how good are my . . . ? I don't quite get the question." She reached over to the recorder on the table and pushed the "Stop" button.

64

"If your legs are quite strong, I'll put you on Clancy. If not, Golden Girl should fill the bill."

Brendan half rose from his chair. He reached over and captured Lisa's slim hand in his own large fingers and pulled her up to stand opposite him.

"I mean, Miss Brenda Starr, that's enough reporting for today. I can't abide sitting still and talking about myself for hours on end. So we'll do a little bit of sightseeing . . . on horseback. Do you ride?"

Lisa smiled, ever so faintly. "In a taxi . . . ?"

He laughed. "Then you've missed one of the finer pleasures in life. Why don't you change? Jeans and tennis shoes with thick socks are fine. And we'll meet at my car in . . . ten minutes? The stables aren't far."

Lisa found herself nodding vaguely at his departing figure. Horseback riding! What she knew about the equestrian arts could fit into a leather stirrup with room left over. Well, she was about to take a crash course. . . . Brendan wouldn't expect her to be a champion rider . . . at least for the first five minutes.

She wondered if he orchestrated everything this boldly. Lisa had to give him credit, though. He had ended the interview precisely when *he* wanted to and then proceeded to plan the rest of her day so that she had little time to reflect on his answers. On the positive side, she reasoned, she must still be in his good graces. One doesn't invite one's enemy horseback riding. Or did one? Perhaps this was his punishment for her asking too many uncomfortable questions.

Lisa shook herself out of the suppositions and hurried to her room to change once again.

Half an hour later she was sitting in a leather western saddle atop Golden Girl, a beautiful buckskin mare. Brendan hoisted himself onto Flyaway, a somewhat skittish black colt that stood a good twelve inches taller than her mount.

"I'm glad it's *your* horse that's named Flyaway, and not mine," she said as they started out of the paddock area. She hoped her flippancy masked the nervousness inside her. She felt the familiar jitters again, when her rational self gave her body instructions and her reflexes refused to obey. Instead they marched to a different drummer, one with a very odd cadence. To be uncoordinated, she thought for the hundredth time, was just as difficult to deal with now as it had been in college. In those days she had chosen books over field hockey and tennis and volleyball. Her mind, she could rely on; her body betrayed her in the most annoying ways at the most inopportune times.

Her thoughts were broken by Brendan's chuckle as he watched her.

"Golden Girl is used to beginners," he said. "You'll do fine. Just remember what I told you. Hug her with your legs for balance . . . and pretty soon you can let go of that saddle horn you're hanging on to for dear life."

"You promise you'll pick up the pieces when I fall?" Lisa said it jokingly, but inwardly she was quaking with, if not fear, then an advanced case of the jitters. She reasoned that Golden Girl must sense this and was at this very moment plotting her overthrow.

"Every one of them," Brendan promised, attempting to rid his face of the grin that threatened to spill out. "Try not to 'steer' so much with the reins. She's not your Chevrolet, you know."

"I surmised as much after I pushed on the saddle horn and she failed to honk," Lisa replied dryly. Honestly, did he think she was totally incompetent? Lisa resolved to show him that she could master the challenge posed by Golden Girl. If Brendan respected her for her riding, she reasoned, perhaps he would come to respect her writing as well.

Brendan took the lead along a narrow trail that led

into the woods. Golden Girl followed Flyaway easily and Lisa began to relax. She was feeling a bit more comfortable in the saddle. Holding the reins in her right hand, she cautiously unwrapped her other hand from the saddle horn and rested it on her thigh. Did one have to be raised in the saddle to look as comfortable as Brendan did astride Flyaway?

"How many years have you been riding?" she asked the straight-backed figure ahead.

"Just since I retired from racing," he answered over his shoulder. That exploded her theory. Well, if he had learned so easily, so could she.

She concentrated on sitting straight, hugging Golden Girl with her legs. She glanced ahead at Brendan. He sat tall in his saddle, his muscles taut within his navy blue T-shirt. His thighs wrapped easily around Flyaway's flanks, tensing occasionally as the horse wound its way along the path. Funny, Lisa thought, but Brendan gave off the very same kind of cool, collected aura as he had done that night at Roulette. He was a man who was at home in any setting.

"Are you ready for the next step?" Brendan called. "I'll take Flyaway into a trot. . . . Girl should follow, but if she doesn't, just nudge her with your heels."

"Ready when you are!" Lisa gritted her teeth, and was glad she had done so as her horse picked up the pace behind Brendan's. She felt as though every bone in her body would loosen from its joints and come unhinged as Golden Girl trotted unconcernedly along the path. Lisa grabbed the saddle horn again, like a shipwreck survivor who spies a life raft floating by.

"Got the hang of it?"

"I . . . think . . . so!" It was all Lisa could do to get the words out between her clenched jaws. Her breath was coming in ragged gasps.

She remembered Brendan's advice about hugging the

horse's girth with her legs. She squeezed her legs tighter, tighter. To her surprise the motion became a bit more bearable, and she released her grip on the saddle horn.

Brendan glanced back and smiled at her progress, giving her the thumbs-up signal. Lisa felt like a first-grader who has learned to spell her name correctly. Amazing, she thought, what a show of praise will do for one's self-esteem. She was contemplating entering the Grand National in England. . . .

"Follow my lead . . . you're doing fine!" Brendan shouted over his shoulder. "We'll do a slow canter now."

Lisa's horse switched from its jackhammer-like trot to a canter. They were moving faster now, but the pace was somehow easier to bear, at least by Lisa's reckoning.

They came to a fork in the trail. Brendan twisted in his saddle to tell her, "Don't let Girl go left . . ."

But he was too late. Golden Girl knew exactly where she was heading. Lisa pulled back on the reins, but Golden Girl was having none of it. Before Lisa knew it, the horse was cantering down a trail lined by trees with low-hanging branches.

"Stop! Whoa!" Lisa commanded. She might as well have been shouting at a speeding locomotive, for all the heed the horse paid her. Branches whipped menacingly at Lisa's face. She held her free arm across her cheek and forehead, and crouched low in the saddle. The branches struck her bare hand and forearm. She closed her eyes and sent a quick prayer skyward.

"Whoa, girl!" It was Brendan's voice. She looked over to see him beside her on Flyaway. He had Golden Girl's reins in his right hand and was pulling both horses to a halt.

"Are you okay?" His look of concern was unmistakable. "Let me see your hand." He inspected several scratches that had begun to swell to an angry red.

The pounding in Lisa's chest began to slow. Now it

was just a steady, rhythmic thumping, only about twice as fast as normal.

Brendan released her hand. "I don't think the damage is too severe. A little iodine should fix you up. C'mon down from there . . . we'll walk to the clearing."

Brendan dismounted and came to stand in front of her left stirrup with his arm extended to help her.

Rather shakily, Lisa stood in the stirrups and swung her leg across Golden Girl's rump. Brendan caught her as she kicked out and jumped to the ground. His arms encircled her waist. Lisa was suddenly conscious of the overwhelming maleness of him. A light film of perspiration blanketed them both. Lisa's blouse stuck to her skin and it seemed as though Brendan's shirt was nonexistent. She could feel the outline of every inch of muscle, his every ounce of rock-hard flesh through the thin fabric. The steady pump, pump of his heart seemed to generate an accelerated pounding in her own chest.

His eyes met hers for one brief instant. They were filled with concern and something else . . . something that reminded Lisa of the rooftop at Roulette and the kiss that had obliterated all else. . . .

But that was crazy, Lisa told herself sternly. Now they were in a pasture, covered with sweat and grime and, in Lisa's case, a painful crisscross of minor cuts and scratches. This was no place for flights of fancy, wild imaginings that Brendan's interest in her went beyond mere concern.

Lisa twisted in his arms, breaking the spell. She patted Golden Girl's sweat-streaked flank and asked Brendan, with a slightly quivering smile, "Did I give her the wrong signal or something?" She paused to catch her breath. "It seemed as though nothing would stop her from rushing headlong into the trees. . . ."

"Not your fault," Brendan assured her. "She used to belong to a fellow who lives a half mile or so up the trail.

I forgot that when she gets near those trees, she involuntarily heads toward home. A more experienced rider could have handled her, but you're too green." He smiled apologetically, reaching for her hand. "Let's take a look at those scratches . . . hmmm . . . not very considerate of Golden Girl, was it?"

Brendan traced a scratch that trailed up her forearm. "Just a surface scratch, though I imagine it must smart like the devil now. Does it hurt?"

Lisa shook her head. "Only when my pride touches it."

"That's the spirit." Brendan dropped her hand and patted her on the shoulder.

They walked beside each other in companionable silence, leading the two horses behind them. With each step Lisa became aware of muscles she didn't know she had. An unfamiliar ache gripped her ankles and legs. She suspected that she was in for more than a few aches and pains as a result of the horseback lesson. She was not only "green," as Brendan had so aptly described her, but black and blue as well. Not to mention red, where the tree branches had scratched her. Perhaps, she thought, Brendan was attracted to women with colorful pasts. . . .

She shook her head to erase the thought. Why did she always think in terms of sexual attraction when he was around? He was certainly not the first man who had looked at her in a way that suggested more than professional interest. Why, then, did it seem as if he were the only person who mattered? Charisma, she reminded herself. As a media star, he had that special attention-getting quality in abundance. All the celebrities did. His charm was like a hundred-watt bulb, though. It could be turned on and off with the flick of some inner switch. She would do well to remember that.

They reached the clearing. The stable was still several

miles away, Lisa estimated. She would have to trust Golden Girl one more time.

"Let me give you a leg up," Brendan said. He cupped his hands and Lisa placed her foot in the cradle they formed. As if she were as weightless as one of the leaves on the trees, he lifted her even with the saddle. She swung her right leg over and settled in, even as her body silently protested.

"We'll circle back to the stable . . . at a walk, this time." Brendan smiled at Lisa and chuckled softly. "Do you turn every outing into an adventure . . . or were you just testing my response time in rescuing you?"

"Mostly," Lisa replied a bit testily, "I was hanging on for dear life."

"A worthwhile pursuit," Brendan agreed, his voice mockingly solemn. "Woman reporter lets nothing stand in the way of her story."

Lisa joined in the teasing. "Not even celebrities who try to do away with me . . . during a seemingly innocent horseback ride. I see I'll have to write one of those letters and send it to my attorney. You know, 'Should I meet an untimely death, it's because I came close to the truth . . .'"

"I'll cooperate fully with the investigation . . . from my hideout in the Sierra Madres," Brendan assured her, laughing heartily.

"Meanwhile, the whole sordid business will come out in a *Lifestyle* article. And your fame will grow, despite it all," Lisa predicted.

"Exactly as I had planned," Brendan deadpanned, then became serious for a moment. "Fame . . . it's not really very pleasant, most of the time. And yet, so many people strive for it."

"You never did?" Lisa looked closely at the profile of his face.

"I won't say that the idea didn't hold a certain appeal

for me," he replied. "But it was never my goal. Winning races, yes. Having cameras thrust in my face, no."

Lisa couldn't resist saying, "Not to mention the horrible fate of having dozens of beautiful women flocking around the winner."

Brendan smiled, a bit sheepishly. "A few did manage to catch my attention."

He looked up as they reached the stables. "And you thought the ride would never end, Lisa. We're home, safe and almost sound."

Lisa struggled to dismount on her own before Brendan could help her. A greenhorn she might be, she knew, but a complainer she was not. She would keep up with Brendan and his outdoor pursuits because she had to. Sitting in her room while he was out riding would mean less time with him, fewer revelations for her article. She would keep up with Brendan Donovan, or at least knock herself out trying.

If there was a single muscle in her body that did not ache, Lisa could not pinpoint it. A half hour in the outdoor hot tub following breakfast had given her a semblance of normalcy, but by midday her joints were protesting every single movement. She began to know how the Tin Man in *The Wizard of Oz* must have felt before Dorothy came along to pour oil where needed.

But there was no one to rescue her today. Brendan had driven to Savannah to meet with his accountant, and Russ was holed up in the garage, where he was tinkering with Lisa's Chevy. Her company for the day consisted of Flannagan, who wasn't much interested in hearing her litany of complaints about her aching muscles. The setter did, however, consent to sit beside her on the deck, his head resting comfortably on her knee as she read more Perry Mason.

That was the way Brendan found them at five o'clock.

"I see you've made another friend, Lisa," Brendan said as he walked out onto the deck and pulled up a chair to sit across from her. He nodded toward the dog. "Funny, but Flannagan here doesn't usually take to strangers so easily."

Was she imagining it, or was there a twinge of jealousy in Brendan's light remark?

"I think we were both looking for a little company today," Lisa said. "He's been whining about all the birds he's been chasing—and missing—all day. And I've been telling him about my sore bones from yesterday. We've gotten along famously!"

As if to confirm her claim, Flannagan licked her hand. "And I always thought he was a one-man dog! Flannagan, old boy, you've fooled me all this time!" Brendan laughed mockingly.

The thought that Brendan might be mildly perturbed at this change of allegiance struck Lisa as funny and a smile worked at the corners of her mouth. The cocky race car driver was used to undivided attention and unwavering adulation, even from his dog!

"I do seem to have won his attention, at least temporarily," she agreed.

Brendan took a deep, thirsty drink from the frosty mug of beer he held in his hand.

"You may have more opportunity to get to know him next weekend," Brendan said. "I'll be going to West Virginia."

Lisa sat up straighter, her body tensing at the news. "But won't I be accompanying you? After all, you agreed with *Lifestyle* that I was to accompany you on any trips."

"*Business* trips," Brendan emphasized. "This is pleasure. My former pit crew is getting together for a couple of days to go white-water rafting in West Virginia. Their assorted wives and girlfriends will be along. And me."

"Oh." Somehow, Lisa knew she would have to get her-

73

self invited and that Brendan should think the invitation was his idea. Then she would have the perfect opportunity to see him—and report on him—in another light.

"Sounds like fun," Lisa added, although personally she had her doubts. It sounded dangerous, daring . . . but that would probably suit Brendan.

"Right up your alley," she agreed. "Thrills and spills and lots of excitement."

He grinned and she could tell he was looking forward to the adventure. "But not your cup of tea, right?"

Lisa laughed. "Whatever gave you that idea? Yesterday I was terrorized by a runaway horse . . . tomorrow, who knows?"

"We *could* use another crew member on our raft," Brendan mused, almost to himself. "But it's not something I would want to talk someone into doing against their wishes. The rapids *can* be slightly dangerous. . . ."

"But if the person was willing to give it a try?" The words popped out of her mouth. Lisa didn't know what had made her say them, but there they were.

"Then you may consider this your official invitation. But if you're going to be frightened . . ." Brendan's slight frown was unmistakable.

"Of course I won't," Lisa retorted. Her hands gripped the arms of her chair ever so slightly, and she was aware of the determined tone of her voice. "I can follow directions as well as the next person. The guides will tell us what to do, and we follow their lead. It's that simple."

"As simple as you thought riding Golden Girl would be, I suppose," Brendan replied dryly. He took another long drink of beer.

"A rubber raft isn't the same as a stubborn animal with a mind of its own. Besides, I won't be solely responsible. And I can swim. But"—Lisa faltered, unsure now if Brendan's invitation had been extended out of a sense of

74

duty—"if you would be more comfortable with my staying here, that's perfectly all right too."

Brendan shook his head, his eyes intent on her face, which she suspected was getting flushed. "No, we'll make it a twosome. *If* you promise not to bring your notebook."

Lisa answered with a steady gaze of her own. "I can't guarantee that everything you say or do will be off the record. After all, that's my job . . . to capture your personality and put it down on paper. I wouldn't be much of a journalist if I didn't use every opportunity to do that."

Brendan sighed. He swallowed the rest of the beer, and looked straight at her, penetrating her gaze. "Do what you have to," he said curtly.

He rose from his chair and crossed the deck to the glass doors that led into the Great Room. He turned and looked at her. His expression was solemn. "Maybe, just once, you could drop the Brenda Starr routine and just be you . . . Lisa Taylor. You might be surprised at what could happen."

There was a moment of silence. Then he opened the door and stepped inside the house. A steady *swish* sound as the door was secured behind him.

Lisa looked down at Flannagan, who was now lying at her feet. She blinked rapidly and bit her lower lip until it hurt. Damn, but the man had an infuriating way of stabbing right to the core.

"But I *am* being myself," she whispered, loud enough for no one but the dog to hear. "And part of me is a working journalist . . . a damn good one."

But for one split second she wished she was anyone but herself. She wanted to be one of the carefree jet set, one of the beautiful women who were photographed on the arm of Brendan Donovan. . . .

CHAPTER FIVE

Lisa stared at the raft attached to the shore by a thick rope. It was a bright orange color and was made of some kind of vinyl, she guessed, and it wasn't the type of craft she wished to entrust her life to. Could anything so flimsy protect her against the churning rapids she had already heard so much about?

If Brendan and the others noticed her trepidation, they didn't say anything. They were busy helping their guide load the gear into the raft. Lisa picked up some tent gear for their overnight stay along the river and struggled to get it into the raft. Maybe, she rationalized, it looked sturdier from the inside.

She checked her waterproof watch. It was one thirty. They would be putting out from the launch area in the next half hour. Lisa busied herself, helping with the rest of the gear. At least the activity kept her knees from shaking so visibly.

Fear, she thought, was an emotion that Brendan and his friends probably experienced only rarely, if ever. They certainly didn't seem to have any misgivings about the white-water raft trip. T.J. and his wife, Susie, for instance, appeared to be old hands at this sort of adventure, and the others whom Lisa had met that morning—Tony, Veronica, Reb, and Donna—were enthusiastic about the forthcoming rapids too.

Lisa had tried, really tried, to match their excitement,

but a nagging little voice inside her head kept asking her how, if she couldn't handle a simple athletic endeavor like horseback riding, was she going to handle the greater challenge posed by unpredictable white water?

When Lisa had accepted Brendan's invitation, the acceptance had come more from a professional interest than a pleasure-seeking one. Yet she had been excited at the prospect. When they had landed in Brendan's four-passenger Cessna at the Charleston airport this morning, she had actually been looking forward to the rafting trip. Now, minus one-half hour and counting, she wished she were somewhere else. Back in her New York apartment, even. But it was too late for second thoughts.

"All set?" Brendan approached her, wet suits in hand. They were to bring the wet suits along in the raft, in case they got cold. As it was, the weather and water were unseasonably warm for October in West Virginia. The temperature was already in the seventies and promised to climb higher.

Lisa, like her raftmates, wore shorts and a T-shirt and underneath, her bathing suit. Her outfit was red, and she told herself that she had chosen the color because it set off her tan nicely, not because it could be easily spotted in the water in case she fell overboard.

"Got your paddle?" Brendan asked her. "You'll remember to keep hold of it, if you take an unexpected dip?"

"Don't worry," she told him. "You won't be able to pry it loose from me."

"Good girl."

Lisa smiled to show that the thought of falling out of the raft did not faze her. She wasn't about to show Brendan Donovan that she was afraid and thereby live up to his expectations, formed as a result of the episode with Golden Girl.

She tossed her head. "Remind me to listen to the

guide's instructions about what to do when you fall out. I have a feeling I'll be needing them."

Their guide spoke up then. His name, he told them, was Randy. He had been guiding rafts on the New River, along with the Cheat River, for the past four years. He was a rangy, tanned fellow in his late twenties, Lisa guessed, though it was hard to determine his age because of the full, rust-colored beard that obscured the lower half of his face.

Randy began his instructions by pointing out the various features of the raft. "Throughout the trip," he told them, "I'll be giving you paddling commands. *Follow them*, no matter what. Because if someone begins to 'steer' on me, even a little, it upsets the angle of the raft and the timing of the run. And you don't want that to happen."

No, Lisa agreed fervently, they didn't want that to happen.

"The key to a good run is teamwork," Randy was saying. "If we function as a team, everything will go smoothly. Now, if someone should make a mistake, it's possible we'll have a few swimmers at one time or another." He smiled. "That's why you've all signed liability waivers."

Nervous laughter rose from Lisa, Brendan, and the others.

"In case you go overboard while we're running a rapid, you need to remember four things: First, don't panic. Second, hang on to your paddle. You'll need it in case you're near any rocks, to steer your body away from them."

Lisa gulped and tried to concentrate on his next words. She was entirely sure now that Randy was looking only at her, having pinpointed the crew member most likely to get into such a horrible predicament.

"Third, position yourself in the water so that you're

78

going down the rapid feetfirst. You don't want to hit your head on any rocks, some of which may be submerged so you can't see them above the surface. And fourth, don't breathe until you see the sky. You can get disoriented very easily in these waters, so it's important to keep your wits about you. I'll explain more tips once we're under way. In the meantime, any questions?"

Yes, Lisa was tempted to say, *who will notify my next of kin if I don't return from this trip?* But of course she said nothing. Brendan, T.J., Susie, Tony, Veronica, Reb, and Donna were anxious to get under way.

The New River, Lisa had to admit, was a breathtaking sight. At this point in its journey through West Virginia, it meandered calmly among tall pines. The dark green gurgling water beckoned the rafters as sun filtered down through the trees, breaking forth in full splendor over the expanse of water.

Randy, the guide, positioned himself in the rear of the raft, directly in the center. Lisa climbed in, struggling to keep her balance, and found herself on the right side of the raft, with Brendan in front of her and T.J. behind her. They all perched on low, soft benches that were built into the raft, close enough to the edge to put their paddles deep in the water. Lisa gripped her paddle tightly in her hand. When the guide instructed, "Right!" she followed Brendan's motion ahead of her and paddled. She got the hang of it quickly, and soon she was paddling with deft, smooth strokes.

The raft glided silently forward. There was little conversation while Randy instructed them in the finer points of white-water rafting. Lisa reached down once to test the water, found to her delight that it was warm to the touch, and began to relax.

They had traveled a few miles when Randy said, "Over on the shore, you'll see the town of Thurmond. It's a historic place around these parts. Used to be an old coal town. Nothing much goes on there nowadays, but a lot of legends have grown up around it here in Appalachia."

Lisa and the others in the raft swiveled in their seats to get a good look at Thurmond. Starting ten yards or so from shore there was a string of deserted shacks, colored the lonely, unpainted gray that was common to abandoned towns. A dilapidated dock hung grimly on to the banks of the New River. A dirt road meandered up past the shacks and was lost somewhere in the woods beyond.

Lisa shivered in spite of the sun that beat down on her back. Imagine, she thought, living in a town like Thurmond at the turn of the century. Making your living in a coal mine. Fishing in the river for Saturday night dinner. The vision of that life took hold of her imagination. Would *Lifestyle* be interested in an offbeat piece about the abandoned towns of Appalachian coal country, and the legends that sprang up around them? She just might convince Marge Kent of the idea. . . .

Before long they drifted out of sight of Thurmond. Talk on board the raft died down, and Lisa was content to listen to nature's sounds: bluejays calling in the woods that lined the shore, water gently lapping against the rocks that cropped up occasionally in this calm stretch of the river. The sun's bright rays struck down with determined force.

Lisa focused her gaze on Brendan's broad back. He had abandoned his T-shirt, as had the other men aboard the raft. A light, barely discernible dusting of freckles ran across his shoulders. His muscles rippled beneath his flesh with each stroke of his paddle and his skin was toasted a pleasing shade of caramel. The tendons of his neck bulged slightly with each move he made. Droplets of sweat glistened along his neck just beneath his hairline and Lisa resisted the urge to reach forward and brush them away.

Brendan's physical presence, as always, had taken hold

of Lisa's thoughts. Charisma, she reminded herself. But then she had to be honest and admit that he was a sexually compelling man, the kind who gives off an aura of sexuality without being aware of it . . . or its dazzling effect on the women around him.

Lisa took a deep breath and tore her eyes away from him, to the water around her. It wasn't any good to get this wrapped up in a man, let alone an interview subject. Nothing but disappointment, she told herself, would come of fantasizing about Brendan. Remember the heartache of the affair with Steve . . . the other women . . .

She was jolted from her thoughts by their guide. "It's time for a swim, folks. Who's ready?"

Shouts of assent went up from the crew on board the raft.

"We're coming up on Fire Creek," explained Randy. "It's a place to swim and a chance to relax before we hit the first rapids."

The Fire Creek "pool" glistened an invitation to the perspiring crew. Lisa and the other women quickly stripped off their shorts and T-shirts down to their bathing suits, not an easy feat when sitting in a wobbly raft. Shoes came next. Then Lisa pinned her hair in a topknot so it wouldn't get wet.

Orange life jackets were offered to anyone who wanted one, but Lisa declined. She *could* swim passably, after all, even though she would never rival Esther Williams. She wanted to show Brendan that she wasn't the total greenhorn he thought her to be. Besides, the courage that had deserted her at the first sight of the raft was gradually returning as the afternoon wore on. Bring on the rapids, she thought; surely this peaceful water at Fire Creek meant that nothing too awfully ferocious awaited them.

They dove and jumped into the water, one at a time and Randy joined them after he had secured the raft.

Brendan swam up beside Lisa. "Having fun?"

81

"It's wonderful!" enthused Lisa, treading water with her feet and hands.

"I'm glad you're enjoying yourself, Lisa." Brendan grinned engagingly. "Earlier, you looked as if you weren't sure you wanted to go through with this. There's still time to change your mind, if you want to."

"Of course not," Lisa answered, breathing fast with the effort of staying afloat. "If these other women can do it, there's no reason I can't."

"Your choice, remember. I hope you feel the same after the rapids."

"I'll let you know," promised Lisa. She giggled. "If I'm still aboard the raft to tell you about it."

Brendan was very close to her in the water and reached out to encircle her waist beneath the water. She felt the familiar clamoring in her chest.

"If anything happened to you . . ." Brendan began in a voice that held a trace of huskiness.

"I'll be careful," Lisa promised, surprised at his show of concern. His hands on her wet flesh were distracting enough without this sudden indication that Brendan had more than a superficial interest in her well-being.

Brendan released her then. It was as if he was suddenly aware of their closeness to each other. He grinned devilishly. "If anything happened to you, as you said, there *is* that letter you were going to file with your attorney . . . in case of accident, and all that. It would cause a hell of a scandal."

Lisa grinned back at him. "I'm sure your former pit crew would stick up for you. They're a nice bunch."

"Good friends to have," Brendan acknowledged. "They've all found other jobs with other drivers on the circuit, but we still keep in touch."

Lisa glanced toward the raft. The others, including Randy, were climbing back in.

"If we want to stay with them, we'd better swim back."

She matched Brendan's slow breaststroke as they made it to the far side of Fire Creek to where the raft floated. Once on board, they quickly toweled themselves dry. Lisa struggled into her shorts and stretched her T-shirt over her head. She loosened the knot of hair, brushing it out with her fingers so that it fell in full, soft waves about her face. Last came the shoes, and she tied the white laces quickly as the raft got under way.

They paddled easily down the river for a time, giving Lisa the chance to catch her breath after the swim in Fire Creek.

Randy spoke up. "Everyone . . . see that bit of white water kicking up ahead of us? That's Surprise Rapids."

Lisa craned her neck to see past Brendan. Yes, there it was, a wisp of frothy water, about a hundred yards upriver. *That* was what she had been afraid of? Why, that was no more threatening than the little churning of water at the bottom of the big athletic club pool slide on Long Island!

"Keep paddling!" Randy urged them. They glided closer and closer to the churning water of Surprise Rapids, the rapids' roar reaching their ears. Lisa held her breath, almost forgetting to exhale. This was no pool, no harmless turbulence, after all. The water ahead moved fast and furiously as they entered the swift, swirling current.

"Everybody dig!" shouted Randy.

Lisa positioned her paddle deep in the water as she had been instructed, lifting it out and back in with as much strength and sureness as she could muster. The rapids lifted their raft up, then down, down, down, and Lisa struggled to keep her balance. Her right foot was hooked —wedged, really—beneath the rubber on the side of the raft, to hold her in. The muscles in her legs tensed with the effort. Water rose up all around them, crashing again and again into the raft to drench them all. Lisa's stomach lurched and she felt a weightlessness inside.

It was like riding a roller coaster. And it was exhilarating! Despite the threat of danger Lisa found herself enjoying the experience. She felt light-headed, unfettered. If this was a roller-coaster ride, she never wanted to get off. And to think she had settled for the merry-go-round all this time! Shouts of "Wow!" and "Whooee!" from the other raft members told her that the others were enjoying the sensation as much as she.

"Right!" yelled Randy above the noise of the rapids, and Lisa paddled with renewed purpose.

"Left!" There, she could rest and catch her breath while those on the left side paddled mightily.

"Everybody!"

A few seconds more and they were out of Surprise Rapids.

"Now you know why we call it Surprise," Randy explained, laughing. "Left, paddle!"

They guided the raft to a calm spot on the river.

"It's bailing-out time," their guide explained. He handed rubber pails to each of them. Lisa hastily scooped up the water that swirled around her ankles and tossed it overboard. This action was repeated again and again by everybody, until most of the water was emptied.

"That was good teamwork on Surprise," Randy praised, "especially for your first rapids. But you need to keep in mind that when I say 'dig,' that means everybody . . . Veronica!"

Veronica, who sat to the left behind Lisa, blushed. "I thought Tony was strong enough for both of us," she confessed.

The others laughed and Randy explained, "It doesn't work that way. Everybody has to do his part . . . no faking. Agreed, everybody?"

84

"Agreed!" they said in unison.

"Okay, the next few miles are fairly easy. Just paddle when I tell you to. Mostly, I want you to catch your breath before we get to the next set of rapids. 'Surprise' was just a baby compared to the Upper Railroad, which is where we're headed. But now that you've got your feet wet and the rest of your body as well, we should be an even smoother team." Randy chuckled.

Lisa unwedged her foot from the rubber seat in front of her and stretched both legs out as best she could. She twisted her back slowly to the left and right, to get the strain out. She extended her neck back, and back still farther, until she looked straight up at the sky. Rafting through the rapids was different from riding a roller coaster after all, she thought. The former activity took a lot more work and was considerably more tiring.

She paddled occasionally as their guide instructed, and let her thoughts drift along with the raft. She had missed a great deal, she decided, by being such a bookworm during her growing-up years. The outdoors held a bounty of precious gifts and she had unwrapped very few of them. This river, for instance. So peaceful, so pristine. Civilization had barely touched its beauty. Lisa reflected that here, one could easily forget about deadlines and reluctant interviewees. It was that kind of place, at least between the rapids. But the respite was over.

"Let me tell you a little bit about Upper Railroad before we reach it," Randy said. "Nobody knows who gave it that name, but whoever he was, he had good reason. You could compare it to a runaway locomotive . . . without benefit of tracks. And you'll know once you're in it. It gathers up steam like it was runnin' down the side of a mountain."

Murmurs—half of them lighthearted, the other half nervous—were heard from the raft's crew.

"Now, all you have to do with the Railroad is remember one fact: You're the engineer," Randy instructed. "Or rather, as a team we work like one engineer. We've got to pull together . . . listen to the commands, 'cause the Railroad takes considerable manpower. You've got to give it everything you've got to blast through a big hydraulic—whirlpool, to you—that sits between two small holes—the lower spots in the rapids. Everybody who's with me, raise your paddle!"

Lisa and the others did as he asked. She was looking forward to Upper Railroad and the exhilaration that came with the successful navigation of these rapids. She wondered if Brendan felt the same.

For the first time she had an inkling of the emotions that accompanied automobile racing. Those expensive machines roared around the track at well over two hundred miles an hour. All that separated the driver from disaster were reflexes, instinct, and a bit of brightly painted fiberglass that could crumple in the blink of an eye. But the thrill of mastering such speeds was the lure that ensnared each driver, race after race.

Lisa wondered if white-water rafting and the thrills that accompanied it caused Brendan to long for the track. Or did this excursion seem to him like a poor second best? It was difficult to tell from his demeanor. He was enjoying himself, that much was clear. The bright flashes of mirth in his brown eyes, the brilliant smiles that flicked so easily across his much-photographed face, told her more than words could say.

But once she had caught a haunted look, a look that went deeper than the bottom of the New River. It was when they were swimming together in Fire Creek and he had put his hands on her waist. "If anything happens to you . . ." he had said. The look of torment was in his eyes for just an instant, before it disappeared. She didn't flatter herself into thinking that the look had anything to do with her. No, Lisa reflected, it had been the kind of expression one usually hid from others. The look that has seen something it cannot bear to see again. He was remembering Guy Tremaine's accident, Lisa knew. It had been a tragedy, unforeseen and beyond control. The upcoming rapids had brought all of that back to Brendan's mind, Lisa was sure. And now she wondered how often the memories of Madrid tormented him.

Lisa gazed at the paddle she held in her hands, then down to the water it sliced through now with clean, precise strokes. The routine motion—in, down, back—was comforting somehow. *Enough* thinking, she admonished herself. *You do too much of that sometimes. Analyze everything till it threatens to burst at the seams.*

"Hey, wherever you are, come back and join us!"

Brendan had turned around from his perch on the bench in front of her. He snapped his fingers before her eyes, as if to shake her back to the present.

Lisa returned his smile with a rueful one of her own. "Sorry . . . I was just telling myself I daydream too much." Stretching the truth slightly, she wasn't about to reveal to Brendan that she had been lost in thought about *him.*

Brendan winked at her conspiratorially and leaned closer. He glanced over at Veronica. "I hope our guide made the intended impression on her. If we don't make it through Upper Railroad, she'll have the devil to pay with Tony!" Brendan chuckled softly and patted Lisa's shoulders. "And you . . . paddling like a pro! I suppose next week you'll want to try the Colorado River? No more of this small stuff then," he kidded.

"The 'small stuff' is just fine, believe me," Lisa assured him. Nevertheless a warm flush crept up her neck. She knew it was ridiculous that such offhanded praise for her rafting skill should warrant such a reaction, but she couldn't help it. She did feel absurdly proud of the fact that, so far, she had mastered the white water without making a false move. *I may not be able to control Golden Girl,* she thought, *but at least I can maneuver a raft.* She was beginning to feel less like a greenhorn and more like an old hand at adventure.

She heard a faint, gurgling noise coming from up ahead. Upper Railroad!

"Get ready," Randy warned his crew.

Lisa and the others poised alertly for the onslaught of the rapids ahead. The noise of the churning water surrounded the crew within seconds. It was like being in the middle of a waterfall as the crescendo reached deafening proportions.

"Dig! Dig!" shouted the guide.

Lisa pushed down on the wooden paddle with all the strength embodied in her hundred and fifteen pounds. She used muscles in her arms she didn't know she had.

"Left!" Lisa paused while the other side paddled. She risked a quick look at Veronica, who was doing her best with a look of grim determination on her face.

"Right!" Bearing down once again on her paddle, Lisa strained to hear the guide's instructions, which were all but drowned out by the roar of the rapids.

They battled the whirling currents of the water. Down, down they spun in the swirling foam. Lisa's head became dizzy at the continuous circling motion and she had trouble keeping her bearings. She clutched at the bench to balance herself.

The rapids were like a runaway locomotive hurtling down the side of a mountain, just as Randy had described. Lisa gasped for breath. She choked as a spray of water came up over the side, splashing her in the face and soaking her hair.

"Dig, dig, everybody!" Randy urged. "We're almost through."

Lisa forced herself to concentrate on the job at hand. She paddled furiously, just like Brendan in front of her.

The raft twisted perilously close to the huge boulders that rimmed one side of Upper Railroad.

There, they were safely past them. The rapids diminished in intensity and their sounds grew weaker with each passing second.

Randy instructed the crew to steer toward an eddy. This was where they would bail out the water that had accumulated in the raft.

"Okay," he kidded, "who wants off this railroad at the next station? Everybody? Ah, you've got no stamina!"

He'd get no argument from her on that score, Lisa thought. She laughed with the others as they bailed out the raft.

She checked her watch. Four hours had passed since they had put out near Thurmond. The time had gone swiftly, like the underlying currents of the New River.

"Now you get to relax," Randy told them. "I'll do what little paddling is necessary to get us downstream to the campsite."

Lisa breathed a deep sigh of relief. The handle of the paddle felt as if it were firmly embedded in the flesh of her palm. Indeed, there were indentation marks on her hand from gripping it so intently. She willed the muscles in her arms and legs to slacken and relieve the tension. And she wondered what lay in store for them on tomorrow's rapids.

After a time Randy said, "We make camp in that clearing past the trees on your right." He steered the raft so that it headed toward a freshly painted dock that jutted sharply from the riverbank. It was a welcome sight to Lisa, who longed to stand up and stretch her legs.

Brendan reached out with a strong right hand and grabbed the first post on the dock. He helped the guide swing the raft parallel to the dock so they could disembark with the gear.

Randy directed the unloading operation. Quickly the

nine of them untied the various wet suits, thermoses, and other gear from their secure positions inside the raft and deposited the gear ashore. The men grabbed hold of the raft and hauled it up the nearest bank, where it would stay for the night.

Lisa surveyed the campsite. Ringed by trees, it contained a dozen or so tents that looked as if they were permanent installations. Remains of a recent campfire at the edge of the woods caught her attention; a large circular area had been cleared for toasting marshmallows, and the tree stumps were placed around an outer rim to provide makeshift seating.

Randy was saying, "As I explained this morning, another raft crew will be sharing the campsite tonight. There is plenty of room for everybody. Four to a tent—but you're welcome to sleep outside beneath the stars if the mood strikes you . . . or if your tentmates drive you out!"

Lisa laughed along with the others. She already knew that she would share a tent with Brendan, T.J., and Susie. Accommodations had been decided beforehand.

She had never slept on one of those narrow, confining cots before. The Girl Scout experience had never been hers, in large part because Aunt Phyllis had a long-standing policy against "skinned knees, poison ivy, and slithering snakes," calamities her aunt was sure would befall a person the minute he or she stepped foot beyond the backyard.

Brendan and T.J. hauled the sleeping bags to the tent and the other men did likewise. Lisa and Susie followed with the backpacks that contained their clothing.

As they made themselves at home in the new setting, the other raft crew that would be sharing their campsite docked their raft and disembarked.

Lisa took a look at them, and realized she must look just as disheveled, tired, and sunburned. She sat on a

90

broad tree stump and rummaged in her waterproof carry-all for a mirrored compact case. Quickly she ran a brush through her long hair, still damp, eliminating the tangles as best she could. She dabbed on a bit of gloss for her sunburned lips. Just because she was stranded here in the wilderness didn't mean she had to resemble a plucky-but-weathered pioneer woman, she told herself.

"Mind if I borrow your mirror?" Lisa looked up as Susie walked over to join her.

Susie added, "Not that it will do much good, but I might as well make the attempt." She ran a blue comb through her short, curly brown hair and handed the mirror back to Lisa. She eased herself down to sit in the shade of a nearby tree.

"Is this your first raft trip?" When Lisa nodded, Susie continued, "I thought so. You did pretty well, though. I think even Brendan was surprised."

"Oh, he had good reason," Lisa assured her laughingly. She related an abbreviated version of her misadventure on Golden Girl. "I'm just not a natural-born outdoors person, I guess," she confessed to Susie.

"Nonsense," the girl told her. "It's all a state of mind. You just have to conquer your fear of the unknown . . . like in auto racing, the only thing you have to fear is fear itself."

Lisa seized the opportunity. "Have you and T.J. been involved in racing a long time?"

Susie nodded. "I met T.J. about six years ago. He was working for Brendan, and they needed someone to keep the books, pay the bills, that kind of thing." She laughed delightedly. "It sounded like fun . . . and it was! Now T.J. is driving and I work with him. He hasn't won a race yet, but he will. And maybe someday you'll be writing about *him* in *Lifestyle*."

There was more than a trace of pride in Susie's voice. Lisa noticed the way her eyes sparkled when she talked about T.J. It must be wonderful, Lisa thought, to have a caring, loving, mutually supportive relationship. For a fleeting moment Lisa wondered if any woman could form that special kind of bond with Brendan Donovan. No, he was too elusive, too independent. Anyway, why was she forever fitting him into a romantic mold? She was, she reminded herself hastily, after a story.

"I'll keep a lookout for T.J.'s name in the sports news," she promised. "In the meantime, I've got this article on Brendan to write. It's not easy . . . he's kind of a difficult person to know, don't you think?"

Susie chewed on a piece of long grass she had pulled from the ground at her feet. "On the surface, he seems very extroverted. But I don't think anyone, in the six years I've known him, has really got *close* to him. Certainly not any of those celebrated lady friends he's always photographed with."

Lisa felt a smile spread across her features. Ridiculous, she told herself. What do you care about Brendan's relationships with the opposite sex? Yet she had to admit that she did care, absurdly so, and she suspected the feeling had started with his kiss on the rooftop of Roulette. It seemed another world away, a century ago.

Back to business, she admonished her wandering thoughts.

"You've probably heard the rumors that he may be returning to racing," she said to Susie. "Do *you* think there is any truth to them?"

"I haven't heard," Susie replied forthrightly, "but that doesn't rule out the possibility. T.J. thinks somebody started those rumors to challenge Brendan to return to the circuit. There hasn't been anyone to take his place in the public eye, y'know." Susie paused reflectively. "The sport does need him right now . . . who knows, maybe he will come out of retirement. I've learned never to be surprised at anything Brendan does."

And I second the motion, Lisa thought.

"Susie!" T.J. motioned her over to where he was standing, near the tent. Susie jumped up and, with a little wave to Lisa, was off to join him.

Lisa quickly dug out her small, spiral-bound notebook and a ball-point pen. She flipped to the first blank page, scribbled the date at the top, and made a few brief notes based on Susie's remarks. She wrote: *Challenge to Brendan? Who's behind it? Check with NY on possibilities.*

"Got all you needed?" Brendan's voice was controlled and very close by, yet decidedly distant in tone. He stood, legs solidly planted and arms crossed, directly in front of her. His long, lean frame cast a shadow across her.

Lisa flushed guiltily and then remembered that she was with Brendan Donovan to write an article, not win his everlasting affection. She thrust out her chin at a stubborn angle. "Susie just made an interesting comment that I decided to check out."

"Wonderful," Brendan scoffed. He indicated the small clearing they were in. "This must be the interrogation room. Let me know if you find out anything earthshaking, will you? In the meantime, try to give everyone some time off . . . they're here to have fun. You know, it's what people do when they're not working!"

He was clearly angry at her for asking questions of his friends. But what did he expect? Lisa asked herself. She certainly wasn't going to ignore the opportunity. And it wasn't as if she had sought out Susie for questioning. "It was a simple conversation, for your information," she said icily. Her blue-eyed gaze refused to drop in the face of his stern demeanor.

"I am not making a pest out of myself, as I promised you before we left Hilton Head," she reminded Brendan. Her voice had taken on a high-pitched tone that she hardly recognized. How this man could bring out the worst in her! "What's more," she continued, "I know

93

very well what 'fun' is. I enjoyed myself today, or didn't you notice? But I've still got a job to do and I'm going to do it. And if that means annoying you, I'm sorry but it will just have to be that way." She took a moment to catch her breath.

Brendan regarded her with an expression she found difficult to read. Then, to her surprise, he burst out laughing. "Whew! You're not shy about saying what you feel, are you?" he said when his laughter had subsided.

"I guess not," she acknowledged a bit sheepishly. "I just thought I should clear the air."

"For miles around," he concluded. "I guess I owe you an apology for my outburst. It's just, hell, I thought you had actually forgotten you were a reporter for just one damn day . . . and then I see you engrossed in your notebook . . . I guess I lost my temper. I'm sorry."

He was perfectly serious now. Lisa thought she would never forget the look on his face, a look that had been rarely captured in photographs, a look he did not casually offer for public consumption. There was a gentleness and vulnerability to it that did not correspond to those qualities she had already come to associate with Brendan: nerves of steel and a heart so heavily armored that all of the beautiful women he had escorted could not break through to reach it.

Lisa swallowed hard. She would have bet her life savings—what precious little there was—that he hadn't said the words *I'm sorry* too many times in his life.

"It's okay," she told him. "We'll pretend it never happened." She smiled tentatively to show there were no hard feelings.

Randy, their guide, trotted over to the clearing. "We need some volunteers to gather wood for the campfire. Any takers?"

"We'll go," Brendan said. He reached his hand out for Lisa's and pulled her up from her perch on the tree

94

stump. His touch was like the sizzle of hot coals on her skin and went beyond her hand to every nerve ending in her body.

But he let go of her hand as soon as she was standing, and Lisa felt a twinge of disappointment. Just because he'd apologized, she told herself, didn't mean he wanted to hold her hand in repentance.

The search for firewood went quickly. They returned to the campfire circle, arms loaded with twigs and branches for kindling. Randy and the other guide soon had built a roaring fire, from which Lisa maintained a careful distance. The pink tinge of her skin meant the beginnings of another sunburn, and the added heat of the fire was uncomfortable.

She looked around the campsite at the lengthening shadows. The sun, which had blazed in the sky all day, now hid low behind a cloud touching the rose-hued horizon. Its light was visible only as a minuscule trace that edged the jagged peaks and valleys of the single cloud.

Meanwhile, the raft crews gathered around the perimeter of the campfire. Lisa savored the aroma of smoked bratwurst as it sizzled over the coals. One by one the campers took a serving of thick buns, supplemented by potato salad and huge, juicy pickles. Lisa poured apple cider from a jug into a paper cup and joined Brendan and the others on a huge log that served as a bench.

Lisa balanced the plate on her lap after she sat down and placed her drink on the ground between her feet, a smile forming slowly on her face.

"There's got to be a reason behind that peculiar little smile you're trying to hide," Brendan teased her. Surprised he had noticed, she nearly choked on her cider.

"I was just thinking there's no better way to satisfy an appetite than a meal by a campfire," Lisa began. "It's new to me, but I could kick myself . . . and my Aunt Phyllis . . . for having to wait this long to try it!"

"You're kidding," Brendan said, looking at her as if to make sure she was indeed telling the truth. "Your first campfire? Where did you grow up, anyway? Miss Peabody's Finishing School for Refined and Proper Young Ladies?"

Lisa chuckled. "Not quite . . . but you're close." She briefly described life with Aunt Phyllis and Uncle Bertram. At first haltingly, then with more candor as Brendan encouraged her, she spoke of her childhood and teen-age years. She managed bites of the bratwurst in between sentences, and Brendan did likewise.

He asked her how she had decided on journalism as a career.

"Easy," she answered flippantly. Yet she knew there was more than a kernel of truth behind her next words. "When you're a journalist," she told Brendan, "you get to examine other people's lives. That doesn't give you much time to dwell on your own."

The truth of that statement was becoming more apparent to her all the time, she suddenly realized, though she didn't say as much to Brendan. Since the unfortunate ending of the love affair with Steve, she had thrown herself into her work and abandoned most social activities. Casual dates had left her strangely numb, and so she stopped putting herself through such senseless encounters. It was easier—on her and her bank account— to pick up assignments from *Lifestyle* and pour her energies into the research and writing of the articles.

When she interviewed her subjects, it was they who revealed bits of their lives, never she. Until now. With a start she realized that Brendan was the first interviewee to turn the tables and ask questions of *her*. It made her uncomfortable and, at the same time, flattered her. He cared enough to want to know the answers, she thought. And then a question planted itself in her mind: *Is he asking me these questions so I'll forget I have dozens of questions to ask him?* The idea was unsettling . . . and it refused to be dismissed.

Lisa concentrated on her potato salad. Its taste wasn't quite as pungent as it seemed before, and the apple cider had lost its earlier bite.

She forced herself to pay attention to the conversation around her. Reb was telling the group of his hair-raising adventures on the Cheat River during a previous white-water rafting trip. T.J. filled in with a more believable version of the adventure, minus the life-threatening episodes, and before long everyone—Lisa included—was laughing helplessly at their good-natured bantering. This gave way to a round of joke-telling that went on well past darkness.

"And now for the entertainment we promised you," Randy announced. He introduced the other raft guide, who was seated on the ground, his back against a tree trunk. A guitar was slung around his neck and rested on his thighs.

Lisa, Brendan, and the others slid down off their log and onto the ground. Lisa leaned back so that the log supported her back, with Brendan settled close beside her.

"Any singers in the group?" Randy prompted. When no hands showed, he said, "Wrong . . . we're all singers tonight. We're starting off with an old Irish drinking song . . . a story of a man and his bride. We'll sing the verse, you'll sing the chorus." At the sound of groans he added, "Don't worry, you only have to sing one word twice— 'aye, aye'—and I'll cue you when it's time."

The guitar player strummed as the two of them sang lustily of the trials and tribulations of the lovesick Irish-man and his bride. Amid much laughter, the chorus rang out . . . "aye, aye!"

Brendan's voice, Lisa noted, was strong and resonantly full. Not Placido Domingo by any stretch of the imagination, but quite pleasant to hear, she decided. Her own singing voice was better unnoticed.

With the first song as the icebreaker, the guides went on to lead them in more sing-alongs. It was, Lisa realized, the kind of fun she had been missing out on for a long, long time.

Brendan seemed to be enjoying himself too. If she had thought he was too sophisticated for this kind of thing, she was wrong. He joined in with the total abandonment he seemed to display in everything he did. Here was a man, Lisa told herself, who was at home in the most sophisticated European restaurants yet also seemed a natural part of the scene in the wilds of West Virginia. Brendan Donovan, she concluded, was like a chameleon. He could change his skin to suit his environment.

It wasn't a conscious act on his part, she knew. Instead it seemed to be an instinctive move that he made with no thought. Would he shed his emotions and acquire others in much the same way? Would he seem to give affection with all the warmth of a summer sun, only to turn into a block of ice and chill that same person with an arctic blast of winter's cold?

Enough, she admonished herself. And she immersed herself in the verses as the chorus of songs continued.

Randy strummed the chords of his guitar and a familiar, haunting melody reached Lisa's ears. It was a popular tune that Steve had once dubbed "our song." Lisa shivered despite the heat generated by the campfire, despite the light sunburn on her skin.

The song brought back memories, painful ones that she had mistakenly thought were buried. Now they rose again, licking at her consciousness like the flames of fire that danced above the coals. Funny, she thought, how the hurt never went away. It just hid and waited, until you were convinced it'd gone. Then it surprised you with sudden ferocity.

98

Lisa blinked back tears that threatened to spill onto her cheeks. Suddenly she could no longer bear to sit with the others, pretending to enjoy the song. With an apologetic little smile for Brendan, she scrambled to her feet. Quickly she stepped backward over the log that had been her backrest. She doubted if anyone other than Brendan had even noticed her departure.

CHAPTER SIX

Lisa headed down the path that led to the dock. She needed to be alone, away from the words of the song that seemed to taunt her. Dry leaves crunched beneath her feet as she hurried along. Once she stumbled and almost tripped on an exposed tree root.

Lisa barely noticed. The song's words of passion never before experienced and of an attraction that was destined to last forever still reverberated inside her head.

What a joke, she thought. The attraction she had held for Steve had been permanent as the clouds that rolled in before a storm. There was passion all right, but once it had spent itself, it dissipated with remarkable ease. Give Steve an introduction to another attractive woman and . . . pffft! He was pursuing her as surely as thunder followed lightning. Lisa had seen it often enough. And finally she had had sense enough to get out from under the cloud before it smothered her. There had been no silver lining in it, none at all.

Lisa reached the dock. She could just faintly hear the music. The last strains of the song died away in the darkness. The sounds of the night—crickets, the occasional hooting of an owl—kept her company.

She walked close to the dock's edge, making out its boundaries in the light of the full moon. Crouching, she settled herself on the grass nearby, her feet just a few inches from the bank.

The world seemed so orderly here, she thought. Things remained much the same, day after day, year after year. Unlike life, which shifted with the tides of an unknown future.

Lisa felt a little bit foolish now. She could hear the campers singing another Irish song. Had she been silly to allow an old song to affect her so strongly? She shrugged her shoulders. It was done now and she was alone on the banks of the New River.

Lisa wondered idly how the river had received its name. "New" was what she needed now in her life, she reflected, as opposed to the old hurt that always squeezed her heart when anything reminded her of Steve.

Once, she had thought she was in love with him. Experience had proved just how easily she could be fooled. The hurt that remained was not from missing Steve, she realized, but from realizing that her heart had betrayed her. Her judgment of men was sorely lacking in good sense.

She stretched her hands out behind her, leaning back on her arms. Her fingers touched a pile of small stones. She picked one up and sat up straighter. She hadn't skipped stones in years, and now seemed like a good time to resume the practice.

Lisa took careful aim and, with a wide arc of her arm and a quick flip of her wrist, threw the stone across the water. It skipped once, twice, making gentle plopping sounds as it lightly touched the water's surface before disappearing beneath the murky depths.

She threw another stone. This one skipped out ten yards or so, light as a feather, before it too disappeared without a trace.

What a wonderful, mindless thing this skipping of stones was, Lisa thought. One after another they flew, each with its own particular destination.

She wondered what destination lay in store for her.

101

Certainly, Brendan would play no part in it. Once her research for the *Lifestyle* profile was completed, she would be far removed from his life. Oh, she might receive a cryptic note after the article was published, but that was all she could expect. And that was fine, she told herself. Why, when that silly song had reopened the wounds from her affair with Steve, was she even *thinking* about Brendan as anything but an interview subject? *Lisa Taylor,* she told herself, *sometimes you confound me.*

Brendan and Steve both reveled in the glare of publicity; both had sought and won the hearts of numerous beautiful women. *And here you are,* she reminded herself sternly, *edging closer and closer to the same trap you recently escaped from. Idiot!*

She picked up another stone and threw it with as much force as she could muster. It skimmed across the river, touching down with staccatolike splashes in a line that was straight as a razor's edge.

A twig snapped, and Lisa's heart jumped.

"That's quite a technique you have there. I knew you'd been hiding something from me . . . hidden talents and all that." Brendan walked to the edge of the bank to stand beside her.

Lisa laughed softly. "I'm a stone-skipper from way back. But don't tell my editor. She's liable to put me onto covering the world stone-skipping contest or some such nonsense."

"Your secret is safe with me," Brendan assured her with mock seriousness. "Mind if I join you?"

"Of course not." Lisa moved over to make room for him beside her on the grassy bank.

He settled himself and his bare arm touched hers fleetingly. She felt as if she had been, once again, touched by one of the glowing embers of the fire. Her skin burned at his touch. Surely, she thought, he must feel the heat and wonder at its source. Her heart rattled against her rib

102

cage. As surely as he must feel the burning of her flesh at his touch, she thought, he must hear the clamor of her heart.

The feeling that had possessed her on the rooftop at Roulette returned, only stronger this time. She tried futilely to banish it. Such feelings had no place in her life right now. But she couldn't seem to convince her body of that. It responded to Brendan like a moth to a flame. And it would light on the flame and glow for a brief, shining moment before the heat became too intense and the moth shriveled into nothingness. But first the moth had to touch the flame, and Lisa had no intention of making the same mistake twice.

"You left the songfest in a hurry," Brendan was saying. "Everything okay?"

Lisa nodded. "The song held a lot of old memories for me. I guess it was silly of me to leave the group like that . . . but, well, I don't always think things out in advance."

"I'm glad to hear we have at least one trait in common," Brendan observed dryly. He picked up a stone in his hand and flung it across the water. It skipped only once before sinking. He chuckled. "It's obvious I don't have your talent in *this* department."

Lisa laughed. "I think you've done fairly well for yourself without it. As for me, stone-skipping is about as athletic as I get . . . right after bubble gum–blowing, of course."

Brendan laughed delightedly. "I could never do that, either, when I was a kid."

"I won a prize at the county fair in Ohio when I was five," Lisa told him. "I still have the ribbon to prove it. But I can't ride a horse, remember."

"You just need practice," Brendan assured her. He picked up her hand and examined her arm. "The scratches have all disappeared, I'm glad to see."

He kept his hand wrapped around hers as Lisa struggled to still the trembling in her limbs. She swallowed and took a deep breath.

"I'm really glad you invited me on this trip," she told him. She kept her eyes steadily fixed on a spot near the edge of the river, as if it held untold mysteries. She didn't dare chance a look into Brendan's warm brown eyes.

"Believe it or not," she continued, "I've been able to forget about work for a while. When you're paddling like mad in white water, it's tough to remember such a thing as a publishing deadline exists. In fact, it's tough to remember that anything else at all exists."

"I know what you mean," Brendan agreed softly. His voice was as smooth as the moss that covered parts of the ground. His mouth was perilously close to her cheek and he was so close, his breathing touched her face. Brendan reached over and, with his forefinger, traced the line of her jaw. "With one exception," he murmured. "You. I'm always aware when you're near me, Lisa, even in the middle of the rapids."

With the slightest pressure he turned her face so it was facing his own just inches away. His lips were tantalizingly close and his nostrils flared lightly as he breathed. Her eyes flew wide at the unmistakably seductive glint in his.

"Lisa," he said. It was all he needed to say. He leaned over and kissed her with tender longing. Lisa felt as though she were swirling helplessly in the middle of one of those rapids. She knew she should do something, anything, to save herself, but she was strangely powerless.

Brendan's roughened hand caressed her cheek, stroking the soft skin beneath her earlobe. His mouth sought hers once again, more intently this time. *Moth to a flame,* her brain tried to warn her. But she refused to listen. Her lips returned his kiss. Her mouth grew soft and full, ripe with wanting him. She didn't care, suddenly, that this was wrong for her, that it held no future. All she cared about was the warm, sweet taste of him.

Brendan's hand stroked the smooth skin of her long neck. Lisa felt his other arm as it encircled her shoulder. Her own hands had found their way to his bare chest.

Brendan . . . Brendan . . . Brendan. Her heart called out his name, and she thought that surely he must hear. He kissed her hungrily, his lips demanding a response that she hadn't believed herself capable of giving until this moment. She opened her eyes only to find his, and she drowned in their inscrutable brown depths.

Lisa quivered as his touch became more insistent. His work-hardened fingers trailed past the hollow of her neck, past her shoulder. She shuddered as they brushed her thrusting breasts. Beneath the thin red cotton T-shirt and bathing suit, her nipples hardened with wanting him. Brendan discovered her arousal. He rubbed his thumb ever so slowly over her breast. It was as though the fabric of her clothing melted from the heat of his desire.

Brendan tore his lips away from hers and groaned, "God, how I've wanted you . . . so close . . ."

Lisa buried her face in his neck and kissed the salt-tinged tan flesh in reply. She didn't trust herself to speak. Every bit of her body was committed to breathing, and this she did with difficulty. It seemed that there was no room inside her next to her pounding heart.

Gentle pressure from Brendan's body caused her to lean back to rest on the grassy bank beneath her. Brendan loomed above her as his chest covered hers. Her bare legs tangled with his and she could feel the silkiness of the golden hair on his muscled legs.

She stared up into his face, above her in the night. His head was framed by what seemed like a hundred brilliant stars. The moon shone its white light as though it had been created especially for them

Lisa's chest heaved as she struggled to breathe. Her

105

back thrust upward, to encounter that delicious electric shock that came with touching him. Brendan's callused hands swept through her long blond hair and his lips traced the hairline at her forehead. At last they found her wanting, waiting lips once more.

She gripped his shoulder tightly, feeling the muscles ripple ever so lightly beneath her touch. His skin was like smooth marble but, unlike marble, warmed to heat both of them as they lay entwined and oblivious to the outside world.

All that existed were the two of them.

Lisa's T-shirt had ridden up on her body to expose her bathing suit–clad stomach. She was vaguely aware of Brendan's hand on the flimsy nylon of her suit. She trembled at the pressure of his hand as it caressed her waist. She longed to feel his touch in every secret place. Reason left her, and in its place was an unthinkable yearning.

Her hand guided the way as he loosened the strings at the small of her back that held her bathing suit together. She ignored the warning bell that clanged distantly in her mind, knowing that this was right for her at the same time that it was all wrong.

He slipped his hand beneath her suit at her waist. She pressed herself against him as his fingers traveled up to encounter the curve of her breast. She felt his breath quicken as he touched the soft, yielding flesh.

"Yes, oh, yes, Brendan," she whispered. Surely he could feel the wild clamoring of her heart.

If she had been able to attach words to the touching and caressing and loving that followed in rapid succession, she would have compared what took place between them to the thrilling and wildly unpredictable action of the white-water rapids.

It was another roller-coaster ride and her heart clutched with each inspired movement. Brendan, skillful, masterful, knew just what to do, where to guide them and

106

when. And Lisa responded, somehow knowing before he did what would please and then excite.

This, this was what it was all about. The longing. The pent-up desire. It all came pouring out of her, into him, and then into her once more.

Brendan's breathing slowed as he murmured softly into her ear. His half words made no real sense, yet his meaning was as clear as the night sky. Their love had been as all-consuming for him as it was for her. His words, the velvet-smooth touch of his lips on her neck, held the world at bay. For a moment.

She stiffened as she heard a sound. It was a rustling of the leaves in the woods behind them. Brendan heard it too.

The spell was broken. He shielded her body with his own. Frantically, Lisa sought to retie the strings of her bathing suit, at the same time tugging ineffectually at her T-shirt.

She twisted her head to peer into the darkness where the sound had originated. Out of the woods strolled T.J. and Susie, hand in hand. The campfire music must have stopped long ago, Lisa's jumbled brain told her. She and Brendan had been oblivious.

T.J. spotted Lisa and Brendan on the bank and said breezily, with his omnipresent grin, "Four's company, I know, but there's only so many places to go around here for a midnight swim."

"Sorry for the intrusion," Susie offered with an apologetic glance at Brendan and Lisa.

Lisa bolted upright. Her suit was more or less intact once again. She was thankful for the cloak of darkness, for it hid her disheveled state as well as the scarlet flush that she knew flooded her face.

But the gleam of Brendan's white teeth was easily discernible. *He's laughing,* thought Lisa in disbelief. Her jaw

107

dropped open as he chucked her playfully under the chin. Then he jumped to his feet.

To T.J. he said, "Midnight swim, did you say? How about currents, pal?"

"The guides say it's okay, just around the bend over here in this inlet. Are you two game?"

Without so much as a glance at Lisa, Brendan answered for them. "We could use a cool swim right about now."

T.J. chuckled. "Something told me that might be the case."

Brendan stood and held out his hand to Lisa. She was still trembling. She wondered if he could feel it as he tucked her hand in his. Wordlessly, he helped her finish retying her bathing suit. The fingers that had touched her flesh with tender understanding moments earlier were now moving in precise, businesslike rhythm to complete the task of securing her suit. Brendan bore little resemblance to the ardent lover to whom she had so shamelessly responded.

The realization slowly began to dawn on Lisa. It was just a game to him, just one night's whimsy, she concluded. Disappointment invaded her body just as thoroughly as the sun had warmed her earlier.

Maybe she should be grateful for T.J. and Susie's interruption. It had quite probably saved her the embarrassment she would have felt had she continued to lie in Brendan's arms, giving voice to her feelings only to hear Brendan respond in casual dismay that he hoped she hadn't taken this seriously.

Oh, but she had. And now she knew she shouldn't have. But that was about all she knew. Everything else about her feelings toward him was a jumbled mess. She shouldn't be surprised at that, she knew. Since she had first laid eyes on Brendan Donovan, she'd hardly known her own mind. She wondered fleetingly if he had had the same effect on the women he had known.

All *those* women. The biting realization hit her that she was just the latest in a lengthy string of Brendan's ladies. *My God,* she thought, *he has mastered the art of seduction so perfectly, he could be the Picasso of lovers.* Tender words, a kiss, a caress . . . and the rest would inevitably take care of itself. And she had been such a gullible victim!

She marched ahead of Brendan with as much dignity as she could summon, not daring to look at him. She wanted to forget the delicious taste of him, erase the memory of the tauntingly masculine feel of him.

When they reached the swimming inlet, Lisa followed close behind Susie as the foursome waded into the water. Aaaahh, that was it. Cool, calm water to douse the fires of passion that still blazed inside her. But they were more like dying embers now.

She swam a short distance beyond the group, her arms slicing through the water with clean, even strokes, her legs kicking with determined agility. She floated onto her back and did a lazy backstroke. She stared up at the sky. The same stars that had twinkled so tantalizingly beyond Brendan's face earlier were still there. But now they seemed to burn and penetrate her very soul with dispassionate intensity, as if admonishing her for being so naive.

She had said good-bye to Steve, she realized, only to fall into the arms of a man who shared his predilection for womanizing. Brendan had bewitched her so effortlessly—carelessly, almost—that she hadn't known what was happening until too late. Her face burned at the memory of the primitive, unbridled response he had evoked in her. She took a deep breath and dove beneath the water's surface. In the depths of the New River, she swam purposefully. Water streamed past her face, its coolness tingling her skin.

When her lungs felt as if they were about to explode, she broke to the surface. She gulped in breath after breath of cool night air. But try as she might, she couldn't expel the treacherously dangerous thoughts of Brendan.

Was she, she wondered, one of those women whom psychiatrists describe as fearful of a successful love life? Those women who, over and over, chose men who were bound to disappoint them. Instead of learning from past relationships, they entered into the next one destined to meet the same unhappy ending, to endure the same endless heartache.

No, no, no! Lisa shook her head furiously and her long wet hair whipped about her face, stinging her cheek, but she hardly noticed. *She* was in control of her life, she reminded herself, not anyone else. Certainly not Brendan Donovan.

"Lisa!" Brendan's deep voice carried over the water. In the moonlight she saw him standing on the riverbank. Susie and T.J. were with him.

"Right here!" Lisa called. "I'll swim in." Within sixty seconds she came close enough to the bank to touch bottom. Brendan offered his hand and she grasped it, pulling herself up onto the grass.

"The Lone Swimmer," Brendan dubbed her, regarding her with a rather quizzical look.

He was wondering why she swam off alone, Lisa realized. *Fine, let him wonder. It's time he felt unsure of a situation for once in his life,* she thought perversely.

Lisa quickly donned her shorts and T-shirt over her wet bathing suit and stepped into her shoes. The others did the same. Single file, they walked back to the campsite and found that the campfire was deserted now. Its once glowing embers had been doused with water. Only

110

ashes remained. Members of the two raft crews were getting settled in their tents.

Any awkwardness she might have felt at sharing a tent with Brendan was dispelled by the presence of Susie and T.J. T.J. handed her a flashlight and Lisa groped inside the darkened tent until she found her cot. It was on the left side of the middle aisle, with Brendan's cot on the other side. A good six feet separated them.

Brendan had had no chance to speak to her alone, and for that she was glad. She hoped that a good night's sleep would clear her head of the confusing, conflicting emotions that were jumbled inside her.

In the darkness, she quickly stripped off her shorts, top, and wet bathing suit, which clung to her body like a second skin. She toweled dry and, sitting on the cot, pulled a white terry-cloth nightshirt over her head. She arranged her shoes underneath the cot where she could step into them in a hurry, if the need arose. Despite the raft guides' assurances that no four-footed prowlers would disturb them during the night, Lisa wasn't so sure. She hadn't totally shaken off her own childhood fears of the wild. In case a grizzly bear poked its head into their tent, she was going to be prepared to run the other way.

Lisa heard Brendan on the other side of the aisle. The cot creaked slightly as his weight settled on it. His shoes made a thud as they landed haphazardly on the floor. Brendan wasn't one to worry about a grizzly bear attack. More likely, Lisa thought, his mind was on other matters. Such as why she was acting so aloof. *If he finds the answer,* Lisa thought, *I hope he lets me in on it.* She knew part of it was because of his casualness, but she also realized that she didn't understand her crazy emotions where Brendan was concerned.

"Lisa?" Brendan's voice whispered her name in the darkness.

"Mmm?"

111

"If you go skipping stones again, how about giving me another try? I get better with practice." His voice was husky and sounded closer than it was.

Lisa knew he wasn't talking about mere stone-skipping, but instead about what had occurred afterward.

She whispered in reply, "I'd have thought you already had plenty of practice at that sort of thing."

"Not in this case," Brendan shot back. "I intend to start where I left off, when we get back to Hilton Head."

Lisa was at a loss for words. What was she going to do when they returned to South Carolina? Pretend the whole thing hadn't happened? Or submit to Brendan's will and regret it later?

She whispered the only words she could utter with any safety. "Good night . . . Brendan."

" 'Night, Lisa."

"See you in the morning," T.J. and Susie answered in unison, in stage whispers.

Lisa blushed in the darkness. They had heard the conversation, of course. But she was thankful they were in the tent. Otherwise she would have spent the night with only Brendan as a tentmate, and she honestly didn't know if she would have had the strength of will to keep her distance.

Morning came with swiftness—and stiffness. Lisa stifled a groan as she swung her legs onto the bare wood planks of the tent floor. Her tentmates had already dressed and gone, and she had slept right through their awakening and departure.

Gingerly she raised her arms above her head and stretched leisurely, arching her back to get the knots and kinks out. She ached all over. Obviously, she thought, her muscles hadn't got the message that she'd transformed herself into the outdoors type. They kept right on protesting as she slipped into a dry swimsuit, a simple black maillot. She stepped into a pair of kelly-green elastic-waisted shorts and matching polo shirt.

She grabbed a mirror and brush, untangling her long blond hair until it hung past her shoulders in some semblance of order. She dabbed on a bit of lipstick and a touch of mascara. Yesterday's sunburn had faded just enough to give her face a warm, healthy glow.

Lisa pulled back the tent flap. Most of the other campers, she saw, were already gathered around the campfire. As Lisa stepped out and walked closer, she saw bacon sizzling in several cast-iron skillets over the fire and breathed in the delicious aroma of breakfast and coffee brewing.

Brendan was carrying two plates in her direction. "I figured you'd be awake by now. How about some food?"

"I'm famished," she replied. Gratefully she took the paper plate and plastic utensils he offered. The two of them settled on a large tree stump. Lisa resolved to put last night out of her mind and get on with enjoying the rest of the trip.

They ate in silence for a few minutes. Above the conversation of the other campers, Lisa could hear songbirds, hidden in the trees. They twittered noisily, as if trying to hurry the campers to be on their way and leave their sanctuary. Lisa heard, beyond the trees, the rushing sound of the New River as it hurried to its far-off destination.

"Sleep well?" Brendan inquired.

Lisa nodded. "Like a log. Didn't even have nightmares about grizzly bears attacking."

"It was their night off." Brendan winked.

He was about to say something more, but the approach of Randy silenced any further conversation.

"If everybody will help clean up the campsite, we'll be ready to go shortly," the guide told them.

"Sure thing," Brendan answered.

113

Lisa took both empty plates to a trash container and, with the others, quickly scoured the area for litter. This done, she joined Brendan, T.J., and Susie in packing their gear. They assembled on the riverbank about half an hour later.

The group settled into the raft, taking the same positions as they had been assigned yesterday. They shoved away from the riverbank and headed downstream. The sun was out and Lisa thought that today might be a real scorcher. When there was a lull in the paddling, she quickly rubbed protective suntan lotion on her face, neck, and shoulders.

She resisted the urge to do the same for Brendan, seated in front of her. The touch of him . . she couldn't even think about it. He may have viewed last night's encounter as nothing more than a fleetingly good time, Lisa thought, but she could not regard it so lightly. Love was all or nothing with her. There was no place in her heart for halfway measures. She reminded herself of the thornier dilemma: separation of her emotions from the job at hand. How could she call herself a journalist and become intimately involved with her subject? Where was her objectivity?

She remembered with dismay the rumors that still floated around her profession about another female writer close to her age. Mention of the woman's name in certain circles inevitably prompted snickers and a juicy recounting of the writer's latest involvement with yet another famous interview subject. No one in the publishing business took her seriously anymore, even though she had once been a promising talent. "No discretion," Marge Kent had once said about the woman, shaking her head in dismissal.

Lisa shuddered at the vision of Marge Kent saying the very same words about her, were she to continue any involvement—however unwisely—with Brendan.

114

She clenched her fists. She would never let that happen. She had worked too hard to throw it all away on an affair that would mean next to nothing in Brendan's mind. Next month he would be seducing whoever else suddenly caught his fancy, and Lisa would be floundering in New York, trying to salvage her professional reputation. *You're too smart,* Lisa told herself, *to let that happen. Use your head!*

She realized that Randy was talking, trying to prepare the crew for the adventures ahead.

"Pay attention, now," he warned them. "See the bend in the river just ahead? After we round it, keep your eyes out for a huge white boulder. We call it Whale Rock."

The crew was silent as the raft approached the bend, and once past it, they saw Whale Rock immediately. It jutted ominously above the water, thrusting upward to tower over their heads as the raft glided by.

"We use Whale Rock as a landmark to alert us to the Keeneys," Randy explained. Lisa could hear a rushing sound in the distance, signaling the presence of more rapids.

"They'll come at you in three stages," Randy was saying. "Upper, middle, and lower. And each one takes special skills, so listen good when I give the signal. Get ready, everyone!"

Lisa tensed for the expected plunge. The Keeneys, she had heard, were some of the toughest rapids on the river. The drop was almost vertical, and navigation left no room for hesitation. She straightened her back and gripped her paddle tightly as they approached the foaming, churning waters.

The raft entered the rapids and within moments was swallowed by its shifting, powerful currents. It plunged downward as water splashed over the sides and the huge waves signaled the approach of the Middle Keeneys.

Lisa didn't have time to think. She concentrated on

following the guide's instructions, knowing that failure to do so could mean disaster. A wall of water rose up on her side of the raft and she screwed her eyelids shut as the foamy liquid washed over her and the others.

Just as suddenly as it had begun, the commotion of the Middle Keeneys gentled and stopped. They were in what the veteran rafters called a "lollygag," a hole at the bottom of the rapids. They were able to catch their breath and bail out the raft.

"That was just a rehearsal," Randy warned. "The Lower Keeneys are the *real* challenge."

Lisa was exhilarated by their success on the first part of the famed Keeneys and couldn't wait for the Lower Keeneys. The rest of the crew was just as anxious . . . except for Veronica, who, Lisa noticed, was gripping her paddle so hard her knuckles had turned white. But there was no time to reassure the frightened woman. The raft headed downriver, its nose plowing into the fury of the rapids. Lisa felt herself plummeting as the raft tumbled downward in a stomach-lurching swoop.

The sensation she felt was one of weightlessness, loss of control. This was how skydiving must feel, she thought. It was exciting and terrifying in the same split second. She wedged her foot tighter beneath the rubber bench in front of her and listened for Randy's commands.

They had entered a V-chute formation in the water.

"Rooster tail!" Randy shouted, and Lisa braced herself for the swing of the raft that meant the paddlers would have to work twice as hard.

All was going well until they reached the tip of the "tail." A gigantic wave broke at Lisa's side, tipping the raft onto its right side. Before the crew could correct the raft's position, another wave crashed over the same side at the rear.

Lisa barely caught a glimpse of what was happening. One minute she was sitting upright with the others in the

116

raft. The next, she felt herself flying out of the raft, and within seconds was underwater. She struggled frantically. The paddle miraculously was still in her hand, and she somehow remembered Randy's warning about hanging on to it at all costs. After what seemed an interminably long time, but was in reality just seconds, her head bobbed to the surface.

She opened her eyes, wiping the water away from her lashes with her free hand. The raft was a few feet in front of her. She caught a brief glimpse of Randy and several others still sitting in the raft. Her dazed mind wondered fleetingly where Brendan, Tony, and Veronica were. They weren't in the raft. Had they been overthrown too?

Lisa had no time to worry about their safety. She choked from the gush of water that broke over her head and engulfed her in the grip of the current. She tumbled downward in the water, and then still farther down.

Feetfirst, a voice inside her was saying. She struggled in the chaotic buoyancy of the water to lie parallel to the surface. She held up her paddle in front of her, none too soon. She felt a jolt as the paddle struck a rock that edged half-hidden just above the water's surface and felt her feet brush against the rough, ragged edges of the sharp stone.

She gasped for breath just before the rapids' current towed her underwater again. *It's got to end,* she prayed in desperation.

As if in answer the rapids seemed to push her back up to the surface, exposing her face to the air and the brightness of the sun.

She didn't see the huge gray rock that emerged from the water ahead. Her paddle merely grazed the threatening hulk, but some inexplicable twist of the current wrenched her body around and her head struck the rock with a sickening thud.

CHAPTER SEVEN

Pain shot through her head. Lisa's hand went up to protect herself, but it was too late. The handle of the paddle that she still clung to was jerked by the force of impact and it struck her just above her right eye. Dazed by pain, she loosened her grip and the paddle was torn from her hand.

She thought she heard a shout from somewhere nearby. But her senses were so fogged by shock and pain, she couldn't be certain. *Stay alert,* she told herself . . . *Don't close your eyes.* For a brief, frightening second she thought how easy it would be to give up. She could close her eyes, and the water would wash the pain away. . . .

Another shout roused her. And she knew she still had the will to fight, if not the strength. Lisa gulped hungrily at the air. Slowly she regained some sense of her surroundings and forced her tired arms to battle the current. Then suddenly its force slackened. She entered a swirling pool of water that signaled the end of the Keeneys.

The pain in her head had dulled to a steady aching. She felt someone touch her shoulder. Strong, steady hands clasped about her waist. She recognized the voice as Brendan's: "Take it easy now, you're okay . . . just relax. . . ."

Groggily, she did as he instructed. She twisted her head once to see his face, which was dripping with water and strained with effort and concern.

"Brendan," she sputtered, but that was all she could manage. She closed her eyes, feeling safe in the arms that gripped tighter about her. She felt herself being pulled through the water. She had no notion of how long he pulled her until something that felt like rubber bumped her shoulder.

She opened her eyes. They were at the raft, and hands reached down to lift her inside.

"Careful, I think she hit her head. There's a nasty cut above her eye," Brendan said as he climbed in after her.

Lisa lay on the dampened floor of the raft as Brendan's face loomed above her. His mouth was set in a grim line and the muscles in his face were tense with worry.

"I'm okay . . . I think . . ." Lisa told him and the others who gathered around her. Suddenly she remembered the brief glimpse she'd caught of the raft just after she was tossed into the water.

"You fell out too . . ." she told Brendan as memory restored itself. "And Veronica . . . Tony . . ."

"All safe now," Brendan assured her. "We were lucky. We went through the rapids on the other side of the raft. You ended up on the rougher side, unfortunately. Here, let me take a look at that cut. . . ."

"It's nothing," Lisa protested weakly. "I hardly feel it at all now."

Randy's voice interrupted. "Keep her lying flat and quiet. She could have a possible concussion. We'll have her checked out at the takeout point . . . it's not much farther downriver."

Lisa nodded reassuringly at Brendan. "Don't look so worried. I've got a pretty thick skin, you know."

"Don't I know," Brendan said, forcing a smile. "Still, it's best not to take chances with head injuries . . . we'll get a doctor when we reach Fayette Station."

"Whatever you say," Lisa acquiesced. She was too tired to argue with him. She was still conscious of the

119

throbbing in her head, but it hadn't gotten any worse. Surely, if she did have a concussion, she would be feeling more pain. But if nothing else would satisfy him, she would submit to a doctor's probing.

They reached the takeout point. Gingerly the men lifted Lisa out of the raft and settled her on a thick cushion of grass near the riverbank. She was embarrassed at the attention. Why, she wondered foggily, did she have to be one of the few who were thrown out when the wave hit the raft, and why had she been the only one to hit her head on a rock? Just when she was beginning to feel quite confident of her skills . . . boom! The rug—or rather, the raft—had been swept out from under her.

And now she had become a burden to Brendan. She was so thankful that he had been in the water to pull her to safety, but now that it was over, his nearness reminded her of her folly. She knew she couldn't have prevented what happened, but she wished to heaven that she was anywhere else right now. *I'll never be the outdoors type,* she thought miserably.

Brendan leaned over and checked her pulse.

Drowsily, Lisa said, "First Golden Girl . . . now this . . ."

"Sshh . . . don't talk" was all Brendan said. He stared intently at her face, checking the pupils of her eyes, wiping gently at the cut above her right eye. She reached up to touch the sore spot, and her fingers came away with blood on them. She wondered dazedly if she would need stitches.

"T.J. . . . got that blanket?" Brendan called out.

Lisa felt the warm scratchiness of wool as a blanket was folded carefully about her, covering her wet clothes.

"I don't need—" she began, but Brendan put his forefinger to her lips.

"Just a precaution," he said. "A doctor will be here in a few minutes. Just rest now and be quiet, promise?" His voice had taken on a softness that indicated deep concern. Lisa looked up into the brown eyes that could so easily melt her heart and found in them more warmth than a hundred woolen blankets could ever provide her.

"Promise," Lisa whispered. She had closed her eyes for just a few minutes when she heard a stranger's voice. Her eyelids flew open and she found herself looking into the watery blue eyes of a gray-haired man.

"I'm Dr. Jamison," he said in a gruff voice. Lisa saw that he was in his mid-fifties, dressed in a navy blue jogging suit.

He continued, "I understand you took a nasty spill. Hit your head on a rock. 'Tisn't the first time I've been called here on somethin' like this . . . you people *will* persist in buttin' heads with Mother Nature!"

"How is she, Doctor?" Brendan interrupted, impatience surfacing in his voice.

"I'll know more in a minute," Dr. Jamison answered tartly. He checked her pulse and shone a small, pen-sized light into both her eyes. His fingers deftly probed the cut on her forehead. Lisa felt like a laboratory specimen that wasn't quite up to standards.

"What's your name?" he asked Lisa abruptly.

"Lisa Taylor," she answered promptly. There followed a series of quick questions—age, birthplace, today's date —that Lisa answered apparently to the doctor's satisfaction. He held up fingers in front of her eyes, and she told him how many she saw. Thank goodness her vision wasn't blurred.

"Feel any dizziness? Nausea?" the doctor asked.

"Not now," she answered truthfully.

Dr. Jamison turned to Brendan. "How were you planning on getting her home?"

"We flew in by private plane," Brendan told him.

"That's out," the doctor snapped. "Cabin pressure and concussions don't mix. How far do you have to go?"

"To South Carolina . . . Hilton Head."

"You'd better find a car and drive, in that case." Dr. Jamison spoke to Brendan as if he were the adult and Lisa a child who couldn't comprehend. She was too tired to protest.

He had taken some ointment out of his black bag and was applying it to Lisa's cut. She winced at the stinging sensation.

"You must remember," the doctor continued, "that a concussion is a potentially serious matter. It's a bruise of the brain and the symptoms may be delayed. I suggest, young man, that you stay here and keep this young lady lying down for at least another hour. Then you can put her in the backseat of a car—keep her quiet, mind you— and drive home. You'll want to see a doctor there. I've tended this cut above her eye . . . looks like it won't need stitches, but the next eight hours should tell. She'll have a good deal of swelling around that eye, though."

To Lisa, he said tartly, "Hope you weren't plannin' on enterin' a beauty contest, young lady. No sirree. You'll be black and blue for quite a spell." He winked at her. "Looks worse than it feels, though. Take my word for it."

He turned toward Brendan. "As for you, young man, just remember my instructions."

"Of course," Brendan answered shortly.

A faint smile softened Lisa's face. Brendan wasn't used to taking orders. It must be testing him severely, she thought, to listen to Dr. Jamison's tone, which seemed to imply that Brendan had been responsible for her accident.

"Get your doctor to X-ray her," Dr. Jamison continued. "You be sure and take her in to be examined just as soon as you can. Will you do that?"

"You can be sure of it," Brendan answered.

Dr. Jamison paused. Looking intently at Brendan, he

122

said at last, "Say, you look kind of familiar. Like I should recognize you from somewheres."

Lisa saw Brendan's body stiffen. She wondered, with sudden compassion, what it must be like to be recognized all the time, everywhere you traveled, to have your privacy threatened at every turn, even in the backwoods of West Virginia.

The doctor snapped his fingers. "You're that race car driver. Donovan. The feller that retired after . . ."

The words hung in the air. Dr. Jamison had the grace not to finish the sentence, reminding everyone of Guy Tremaine's horrible crash.

"Well, I'll be," the doctor went on hurriedly. "My wife brings home every magazine that's got your picture in it. Wait till I tell her—"

"About Lisa, Doctor," Brendan broke in, a bit brusquely. "That bump on her head *is* sizable . . . you're sure it's okay to move her?"

"Wouldn't have told you if it wasn't," Dr. Jamison said, bristling at the sound of doubt in Brendan's tone. "Like I said, I've seen more than my share of accidents on the New River. Haven't been wrong yet."

Lisa carefully eased her body to a sitting position, trying unsuccessfully to ignore the persistent and all too familiar throbbing in her head. Today was one of those jackhammer days in which her brain seemed to be the setting for a relentless drilling, so loud she found it difficult to hear anything else.

She pulled her blue silk robe tighter and tried to get comfortable. If that could be done anywhere, she thought, it was here in the Great Room of Brendan's home. In the four days since their return from the New River rafting adventure, she had become quite used to her surroundings. The soothing earth tones . . . the gentle whirring of the ceiling fans high overhead . . .

123

even Flannagan in his customary position beneath the coffee table . . . all worked a kind of soothing magic on her.

Lisa reached for the glass of water on the rattan table beside the sofa. She took two aspirin from a three-quarters-full bottle in the pocket of her robe. That ought to stop the jackhammers for at least a while, she figured.

Flannagan's ears perked up at the sound of a car in the driveway. A minute later Brendan walked into the room, wearing his usual casual garb of faded blue jeans that hugged his tightly muscled body and a striped T-shirt that defined every inch of flesh on his upper torso. Oh, how well Lisa remembered the feel of him. And how hard she was trying to forget. He carried a paper sack, which he handed to Lisa.

He asked, "How's it going today?"

Lisa forced an optimistic smile. "A little better . . . though you would never know it, to look at me."

Brendan grinned, flashing teeth as white as the aspirin Lisa had just swallowed. "You do look a little bit like the loser in a one-sided fistfight," he teased.

He sat on the edge of the sofa, his thigh nudging her waist. He placed his thumb lightly above her right eyebrow. "It does look as though the swelling has gone down, just as the doctor promised."

Brendan had taken her to see Dr. Jackson in Savannah upon their return from the New River. He had examined Lisa, told her she was lucky she didn't need stitches for her cut, and then dropped the bombshell: she had a concussion, just as Dr. Jamison had surmised. Not a severe one, but serious enough to warrant bed rest for the next ten days.

"But that's almost two weeks!" Lisa had cried in dismay. She couldn't possibly waste so much time, she explained patiently to the doctor. She had an article to write, a deadline to meet. . . . But her explanations had

124

fallen on deaf ears. Dr. Jackson had spoken with Brendan, and the matter was taken out of her hands. She would recuperate at Brendan's home, and that was that.

Now Lisa smiled back at Brendan. His nearness almost made her forget the pain inside her head. "I chanced another look in the mirror today," she confessed, making a face. "Lovely, if you like black and blue with a daring touch of purple. You must have to brace yourself before you see me."

"Nonsense," Brendan shot back, a trifle brusquely. Then he winked. "I'm attracted to women who've got a distinctive look."

"It's distinctive, all right," Lisa muttered.

"Here, I thought this might make you feel better." Brendan reached into the paper sack he still held. His hand emerged, clutching the latest issue of *Lifestyle*. The banner headline read, MAISH LAWRENCE: THE LOW-PROFILE PRINCE IN A HIGH-STAKES BUSINESS . . . *by L. B. Taylor.*

Lisa whooped with delight, then winced as the throbbing in her head reminded her of the concussion. But now she didn't care so much about the flash of pain.

"It's out!" she exclaimed breathlessly as she accepted the magazine from Brendan. "Oh, thank you for picking it up. To think I'd forgotten it was due to hit the newsstands today!"

"Understandable, in your shaky condition," Brendan assured her as he smiled down at her. "By the way, I took the liberty of reading the article while I was stuck in traffic. It's very good, Lisa."

"Thank you." She accepted the unexpected compliment with quiet pride. She held his eyes with her own.

"I might even exceed it with the profile on you . . . if you'll let me."

She was alluding to Brendan's refusal to be interviewed since they had returned to Hilton Head. He had insisted, with the support of Dr. Jackson, that she needed absolute rest. She shouldn't be thinking of her work. But that was due to change with time, she thought, and when the interviews resumed . . .

The corners of her mouth turned up as her gaze locked with Brendan's. "You haven't lived as long as Maish Lawrence," she said wryly, "but I think you've got as many mysteries about you . . . those phone calls from Europe, for instance—"

Brendan interrupted her. "They're private, as I told you."

"But something tells me they have to do with your getting back into racing," she persisted.

Brendan scoffed at her. "Whatever gave you that notion?"

"Certain sources," Lisa hedged. "Now, if you would like to clear the air . . ."

"What I would like, Miss L. B. Taylor, is for you to get well and recuperate from your concussion." He softened the harshness of his tone with a smile. "Then we'll resume our discussion about my career."

"Okay," Lisa agreed. "But you can't dodge me forever."

"I don't intend to," Brendan answered. The look in his eyes was suddenly somber. "In fact, I have a couple of very personal questions to ask *you*."

Lisa lowered her gaze, staring instead at the cover of the magazine as Brendan rose impatiently from the sofa.

"Can I get you anything?" he asked.

"No, thanks. Russ has me all taken care of . . . and Flannagan is here to cater to my every whim." She was forced to meet his eyes again.

"Naturally," Brendan said dryly. He had crossed the room to stand at the passageway leading to the kitchen. "That dog liked you before . . . now that you're a semi-invalid, he's a *slave* to you."

"Do I detect a note of jealousy?" Lisa teased, relieved that the conversation had shifted to safer ground.

"You're damn right." Brendan grinned. "Man's best friend, and he moves in on my girl. . . ." Brendan shook his head and disappeared down the hallway.

Lisa caught her breath. *My girl,* wasn't that what he had said? Don't take it literally, she warned herself. He probably meant nothing by it. *My dog, my girl* . . . Still, the thought that he just might regard her as "his girl" was enough to quicken her heartbeat.

Lisa lay back in the cushions and contemplated the fan going around high above her. Since they had returned from the New River, neither one had brought up that passionate night on the riverbank. If Brendan planned, as he had said, to repeat the episode, Lisa's concussion had prevented any romantic overtures.

Indeed, Lisa reflected, he had been the perfect gentleman ever since. In fact, he had looked after her with solicitous concern. Although he would never admit it, Lisa suspected that he felt guilty because of her injury. He had suggested that she take the raft trip, and Lisa knew him well enough by now to know that for him, this was tantamount to flipping her out of the raft with his own hands. She wouldn't be surprised if he thought her concussion was essentially his fault, ridiculous as the idea was. The man carried about an enormous load of responsibility, Lisa thought. That was one of the facets of his character that contrasted so curiously with his reputation as a playboy. The two images just wouldn't coincide.

But that wasn't the thought uppermost in her mind right now. The truth was, the more she was in the company of Brendan, the more she felt herself irresistibly drawn to him. All the arguments she had marshaled against him after their lovemaking on the riverbank were slowly crumbling in the face of his current actions.

Lisa realized that she had fallen for Brendan, not because of his physical attraction—the very thing she had guarded against—but because of those intangibles that were hard to put a finger on—qualities like kindness, thoughtfulness, concern . . . qualities she never would have thought she would associate with Brendan Donovan.

She sighed a small sigh. If she admitted to herself that she had fallen in love with Brendan, what then? What difference would it make? She would bet that he didn't have the same deep feelings for her. They just weren't in his repertoire, she knew. Oh, he might play the gallant suitor for a time, but then the feeling would wear off and he would seek out another woman on whom he could test his charms. Then there was the matter of her career to consider. Her reputation as a journalist would suffer, as sure as the jackhammers continued to pound in her head.

These thoughts had been tumbling around inside her, unexpressed and unresolved, for days. But Lisa felt she had made some progress. Now, at least, she could admit to herself that she was in love with Brendan. It didn't make her feel any better, but it did seem to be one certain conclusion in the midst of a thousand uncertainties.

She would never have to act on those feelings, or admit them to Brendan. Just recognizing them seemed to be a step in the right direction. That way, she could guard against them.

The telephone rang out sharply on the table beside her and Lisa abandoned her thoughts. She knew Brendan would answer from his workshop, but when the phone rang a fourth and then a fifth time, she picked up the receiver. Brendan was obviously not near the telephone.

"Donovan residence," she answered briskly.

A woman's voice, tinged with a French accent, asked for Brendan. Lisa couldn't help picturing the woman who possessed such a voice as something of a cross between Brigitte Bardot and Leslie Caron.

"I'm sorry, but he's outside just now," Lisa said. "If I could give him a message?"

"Certainly." The woman's voice was just a bit curious, Lisa noticed with a perverse sense of satisfaction. "Please have him call Nina Foy in New York. He has my number. Tell him it's about . . . tell him it's rather important that I speak with him today."

"I will," Lisa promised as she wrote the name quickly on the scratch pad beside the phone. They said good-bye to each other, and Lisa cradled the receiver.

Nina Foy . . . Nina Foy . . . Why did the name trigger a memory? She told herself that her curiosity stemmed from the profile she was writing, but her conscience told her otherwise.

She was jealous. That was the plain and simple truth. And a jealous woman doesn't need reason to interfere with her thoughts. Nina Foy . . . She remembered the stack of tear sheets she'd brought with her to Hilton Head. Was it in one of those articles that she had first read the name?

Gingerly she swung her feet to the floor. She stood and walked slowly on still wobbly legs to her bedroom. The stack of articles she had in mind was in her briefcase, beside the dresser bureau.

Impatiently, Lisa riffled through the contents. Faces of beautiful women came one after another, all on the arm of international jetsetter Brendan Donovan. It was the face of the cool, sleek brunette that stopped her cold. She read the caption underneath: *Brendan Donovan and Nina Foy step out for a rare night at Maxim's in Paris.*

Lisa quickly filed the article back in its place. So, that was Nina Foy. She looked like the kind of woman who could survive a hurricane with every hair in place, Lisa thought, or . . . a white-water rafting trip without suffering a concussion, assorted bruises, and an unsightly black eye.

129

Lisa glanced into the mirror above the bureau, which was a mistake. The contrast between the beautiful Nina Foy and herself was laughable, only Lisa didn't feel like laughing. She leaned closer to examine the bruise that circled her eye. Was she imagining it, or was the black-and-blue coloring fading somewhat? Wishful thinking, she told herself. And even when the black eye had disappeared, she still would never look like Nina Foy, who appeared to have just stepped out of the pages of *Vogue* magazine.

A door slammed inside the house, and Lisa turned from the mirror and walked slowly back into the living room.

"Hey, you're supposed to be resting," Brendan said. He stood just inside the Great Room. "When Russ gets back from his errands, he'll have my hide for letting you walk around."

"He'll never know," Lisa promised, settling herself down on the familiar sofa. Brendan walked around to face her, leaning casually on the back of an armchair.

"By the way," Lisa said, "I just took a phone message for you. Here it is. . . ." She tore off the top page and handed it to Brendan. "Nina Foy."

"Yes, thank you." Brendan stuffed the message into the back pocket of his jeans.

Lisa blurted, "She's very beautiful."

"What?" Brendan's expression was quizzical and slightly confused.

Lisa realized she wasn't making much sense. "Her . . . her picture," she stammered. "I've seen it in a magazine."

Lisa could have kicked herself for the inane words. *I sound just like a sixteen-year-old,* she thought with dismayed embarrassment. Her mouth was dry and her tongue felt like a piece of sandpaper.

Brendan's mouth curved in a smile. He nodded slowly.

130

"She *is* very beautiful, now that you mention it. I don't suppose you detected the resemblance, though."

"Resemblance?" Lisa repeated stupidly.

"To Guy Tremaine. She's his sister."

Lisa struggled to think above the pounding in her head.

"Ohhh. But her name?"

"She is married to a fellow by the name of Jean Claude Foy."

And, as if that explained everything, Brendan turned to Flannagan, who lay stretched out beneath the coffee table.

"C'mon, fella. You must be hungry." The dog followed Brendan into the kitchen.

Lisa sank back onto the pillows. She heard clattering sounds from the kitchen.

You fool, Lisa chastised herself. *Of course, Brendan could see right through you. And what business was it of yours who Brendan's caller was, and what she looked like?* Lisa's cheeks flamed as she realized how her jealousy must have blazed brightly for Brendan to see.

Brendan strolled into the Great Room, slapping his hands on his thighs. "That should appease Flannagan for at least half an hour. I'll be in my office, Lisa, if you need me, or if not there, in the workshop."

Lisa nodded, watching him bound upstairs to his loft office, his long legs taking the stairs two at a time. She picked up her copy of *Lifestyle,* flipping through the pages without really concentrating on the articles.

A few minutes had passed when a strange clattering sound from the kitchen distracted her. Flannagan? She had better investigate. The clumsy Irish setter had an endearing habit of wreaking havoc wherever he planted his considerable bulk.

Lisa entered the kitchen, to find Flannagan wagging his tail. His bowl was tipped and a small pool of water

131

formed at his front paws. As if apologizing, the dog licked her hand vigorously. She couldn't help smiling.

She reached for a towel to blot up the water. As she hung it back on the rack, she noticed a piece of paper tacked up on the cork bulletin board beside the refrigerator.

Brendan, the note read in Russ's handwriting, *Guy has asked about DEC's start-up date. Can you find out anything?*

Lisa's thoughts whirled. Here was some clue, possibly, to the endless number of phone calls that Brendan had received and made ever since they had returned to Hilton Head from the raft trip. Lisa had no compunction about snooping—the message was there for anyone to see, including her.

She studied it again. Guy was Guy Tremaine, obviously. So, Brendan was in regular contact with him, it seemed. But what was DEC? Initials of another person? A company? And what did a "start-up date" mean? And what did Guy Tremaine have to do with it?

She started as she heard Brendan's voice. "Now I suppose you'll be asking still more questions?"

Lisa turned around. Brendan stood in the doorway, his hands on his hips. He was not smiling as he continued, "I thought I heard a noise in here . . . thought maybe something happened to you . . . but you're quite all right, I see. Well enough to read other people's messages, in fact."

His voice was tight with controlled anger. His eyes, Lisa saw, flashed dangerously.

She thrust her chin forward stubbornly and said, "I thought the bulletin board was public domain. And now that I've read your message . . . I'm curious to know what DEC is. And what Guy Tremaine has to do with it. I think," she said in measured, deliberate tones, "it may be important to my article."

132

Brendan fumed, "I don't give a damn *what's* important to your story. This is private business, Lisa. Not for public knowledge."

"Why are you so adamant—" Lisa began, but she was cut off.

"Never mind why." Brendan bit off the words through clenched teeth. "I agreed to a profile in *Lifestyle,* not an investigation so thorough it would rival the FBI's!"

"That's ridiculous!" Lisa stormed in reply. The pounding in her head intensified, but she ignored it. "If you would just be up front and honest with me in the first place, we wouldn't be having this argument. It's this infernal secrecy you insist on that complicates matters. Everything is such a mystery with you!"

Her body, underneath the floor-length silk robe, heaved with indignation. Brendan looked as though he was about ready to move toward her, but he checked himself as she continued. "Why not tell me what's developing with Guy Tremaine? Like it or not, Brendan, he *is* a part of your story. And I'll find out the answers, if not from you, then through other sources. If you would just open up a little more, let *me* be the judge of what is pertinent to the story and what's not. I *do* respect your privacy, believe me."

Brendan laughed hollowly. There was no humor in the sound. "I've heard all the promises before, Lisa, from other 'sincere' journalists . . . with the same results each time. They write what will get them noticed. I have no illusions that you won't do the same."

"Of all the—" Lisa sputtered. "If you're so convinced this will be a hatchet job, why did you agree to the interviews in the *first* place?"

"Call it a temporary insanity," Brendan retorted angrily. "It seemed a good idea at the time." He paused and looked at Lisa with an unfathomable expression in his

133

brown eyes. "Who knows, it may still prove to be advantageous."

He walked to the counter and the instant-coffee machine and very deliberately poured himself a steamy cup. Black, no sugar. A fitting match to his personality, Lisa thought grimly.

She jammed her fists into the pockets of her robe. Brendan sipped his coffee, regarding her solemnly. His eyes, just visible over the rim of his coffee cup, darkened to match the liquid within.

It was a stalemate. Without another word, Lisa turned and stalked to her bedroom, shutting the door firmly behind her. Suddenly the headache from her concussion wasn't bothering her nearly as much as the scene she'd just been a part of.

The gall of the man! If he was using *Lifestyle* for some as yet unannounced end of his own, he was in for a rude surprise, she vowed. She would find out about DEC and Guy Tremaine's involvement, without Brendan's help. If he was expecting a "puff piece" extolling his virtues, he wouldn't get it in *Lifestyle,* Lisa resolved. She lifted the stack of clippings out of her briefcase and laid it on her bed. She settled beneath the covers, propping herself up with pillows behind her back.

With notebook and pencil in hand, she began writing. She had had all the "rest and relaxation" she could handle. Maybe, she thought, getting her mind on the article once again would lessen the effects of the concussion.

But she was surprised when, an hour and a half later, her eyelids drooped one last time and refused to open again. Her brain rebelled at focusing on the pages in front of her. She forced her eyes open again to check the alarm clock. It was only ten o'clock, much too early for sleep. But her headache told her to call it a night. Too tired to even wash her face, she reached over to switch off the lamp at her bedside.

134

How long she slept before the nightmare awakened her, she didn't know. Lisa bolted upright in bed, clutching at the dampened sheets with perspiring palms. The dream had seemed so real! Lisa fought to still her trembling. She swallowed, but her mouth remained parched. Slowly, in fragments, the dream came back to her in all its horror.

She had been in a raft on the New River with Brendan. She had been thrown overboard by a wave. Brendan shouted to her . . . he was on the riverbank. She couldn't make out his words. White objects drifted within her reach. Life preservers! But no, when she reached out to grasp one in her hands, it had turned out to be nothing but a flimsy piece of paper. The next one, and the next, were the same. Paper! The *Lifestyle* masthead was on each piece, and so was a photograph. When she held it closer, she could see it was a photograph of Brendan, each time with a different woman. Lisa had flung the sodden papers away from her, crying desperately for help as she churned her arms and legs in the water.

But Brendan had gone and the riverbank was deserted. She was all alone in the New River. Alone, with only *Lifestyle* sheets, worthless to her now, to keep her company.

And then she had awakened, gasping for air.

Her recovery from the concussion was complete six days later. When Lisa looked in the mirror that morning, she told herself she looked like a human being again. The doctor pronounced her fit, and Lisa returned to her mission: the article on Brendan. The nightmare never recurred, but at odd moments she found herself thinking about it . . . and trying to dismiss it.

Brendan consented to several lengthy interviews, but try as she might, Lisa could not break through the wall of reserve he had built up around himself. Oh, he was magnanimously informative about dozens of inconsequential things, but infuriatingly silent on the subject of Guy Tremaine and DEC. Lisa vowed to ferret out the truth some other way. She wasn't going to turn in an incomplete article to Marge Kent, after the editor had shown such faith in her ability to get the real story on Brendan Donovan.

Brendan kept his distance, in both the interview and his relationship with her. He had mentioned offhandedly during one of the interviews that he carved wood in his spare time. When Lisa expressed interest in seeing his work, she wasn't prepared for what she saw during their minitour of his workshop. Beautifully crafted in the rich, mellow tones of soft teakwood, figures of pelicans, swans, and other wildlife populating the coastal regions of the South were handsomely carved and unobtrusively marked with Brendan's distinctive initials.

None of the carvings were for sale, Brendan told her. He explained that he didn't want to turn a pleasure into a duty. Instead, he gave them as gifts to friends.

Lisa made a hasty note that at least one of these wood carvings should be photographed for the *Lifestyle* article and decided to ask the magazine to send a photographer in the next week or two.

Brendan was obviously dedicated to his art and Lisa thought, with a twinge of dismay, that her vivid imagination had been working overtime again. She had thought that Brendan was purposely avoiding her by spending long hours in his workshop, but even her untrained eye could see the perfection of these wood carvings could be achieved only with hours of concentrated work.

When Brendan told her he was leaving Hilton Head to retrieve his plane, still in West Virginia, Lisa breathed a sigh of relief. The underlying tension in the house had not abated since their argument about the note concerning DEC and Guy Tremaine, nor in their interview ses-

136

sions. Brendan had been almost formal with her, in fact, as though he didn't want to unlatch the gates that held back his emotions.

Lisa was content to leave things as they were. Somehow, she knew, their hotly expressed differences over the content of his *Lifestyle* profile had driven a solid wedge between them. She didn't know if it could ever be removed, or if it were, at what cost.

Before he left, Brendan urged her to "walk the beach, go sight-seeing, anything you have a mind to do" while he was gone. Lisa needed just one more session with him to wrap up her interviews, but it would have to wait until he returned. In the meantime, Lisa vowed, she would take him up on his suggestion. Although it wasn't quite the activity he had in mind, Lisa had a surprise in store for him. It had to do with Golden Girl.

She broached her idea to Russ the evening before Brendan's departure.

"Do you suppose," she asked the older man, "Brendan would mind if I took a few more riding lessons on Golden Girl?"

" 'Course not!" Russ assured her in his usual gruff manner. The two of them were sitting in the kitchen sharing samples from a batch of freshly baked brownies.

"Heck, he'd be glad to go with you himself if he wasn't going out of town," Russ said.

"That's just it," Lisa said quickly. "I don't want him to know about it . . . not just yet, anyway."

Russ was puzzled. "You want to explain that one, young lady?"

"I'm not sure I can . . . but if he wasn't to know about it until after the fact, I think I would do better with Golden Girl," Lisa said. "It would take the pressure off . . . the feeling that I was letting him down again if I should fail." She laughed ruefully. "There's no telling *what* Golden Girl will decide to do with me this time."

Russ patted her hand reassuringly, his gnarled and callused fingers covering her own small, tapered ones.

"There, girl, that's no attitude. But I thought you'd had your fill of ridin'."

Lisa grinned. "Almost." Her blue eyes deepened as she explained to Russ, "It's just that, well, right now I feel a need to accomplish something. I mean, my first horseback-riding session was a disaster, the raft trip resulted in a concussion . . . even my article refuses to get off the ground!"

Russ nodded knowingly. "I think I see what you mean."

With a glance in the direction of Brendan's workshop, which was safely out of earshot, he said with a conspiratorial twinkle in his eye, "We'll go over to the stables first thing in the mornin'."

"But I don't want *you* to have to go to any special trouble," Lisa said.

"No trouble. Who d'ya think taught Brendan to ride when he was just knee-high to a whisker? It would be a pleasure for me, Lisa."

Lisa beamed. It was the first time Russ had addressed her as anything but "young lady" or "girl." Now, if she could just convince Golden Girl to treat her with as much courtesy . . .

She needn't have worried. Under Russ's careful, patient tutelage she made considerable progress with Golden Girl on the first day. On the second day, Russ urged her to face the orchard and the low-branching trees that had been her nemesis.

"You've got to be able to control your horse so it knows you're the boss. You're a quick learner, Lisa. You're ready," he'd told her.

So, with considerable trepidation, Lisa set off for the orchard. Her fingers stiffened on the reins as Golden Girl neared the site of the mishap, but she forced herself to concentrate on Russ's careful instructions. Half an hour later she cantered back to the stables, where Russ was waiting.

He nodded approvingly. "That big ol' smile on your face tells me what I wanted to know. Everything go okay?"

"Terrific!" exalted Lisa, patting her horse's neck. She swung her right leg over the saddle and slid to the ground in one fluid motion. Impulsively, she gave Russ a kiss on the cheek. "Thank you so much!"

Russ ducked his head and kicked the toe of his boot at an imaginary object on the ground. He was uncomfortable, Lisa knew, at this unexpected display of affection.

"Wasn't nothin' I did. You near taught yourself, young lady!"

Lisa smothered a grin. *So we're back to "young lady" now,* she thought, amused.

Brendan returned that night, long after Lisa had retired to bed. When she awoke in the morning, she dressed in tailored blue jeans and white boat-necked blouse, and strolled into the kitchen.

Brendan and Russ were already eating breakfast. A picnic basket, packed with thick roast beef sandwiches and two thermoses, sat conspicuously on the counter.

"There she is!" Russ boomed, a shade too heartily for that hour of the morning, to Lisa's way of thinking.

"I was just tellin' Brendan, it's a glorious day for a picnic! Yessir! Thing is, I have to finish that durn tune-up I promised old Mrs. Wilson down the road. But you two . . ."

Brendan glanced at Lisa, then at the picnic basket and back at Lisa. "We could finish the interviewing this evening . . . or during the picnic."

"We could," Lisa agreed nonchalantly. She knew that Russ had set up the picnic scenario for a purpose.

139

Russ began setting a place at the table for Lisa. "Good, then, it's all settled."

If Lisa hadn't known better, she would have thought Russ was playing matchmaker.

Brendan glanced at Lisa. "Where would you like to go? The beach?"

Russ cleared his throat. "That's the other thing I wanted to mention to you, Brendan. I thought you might want to visit the cabin today." Turning to Lisa, he explained, "I've had it for years—just a ramshackle place it is, up in the hills." Then, looking at Brendan, he continued, "Old man Hayes in the cabin down the road from it wrote me that he thought there might be some roof damage from the last storm. If you wouldn't mind . . ."

Brendan chuckled. "I wouldn't mind, Russ. But maybe Lisa would."

Brendan explained to Lisa as she sampled the toast Russ had placed in front of her. "The cabin is in a pretty remote spot. The best way to get there is on horseback. Even then, we'd have to drive a couple hours to the path that leads up to the cabin, and trailer the horses. I don't imagine you're too keen on spending the day with Golden Girl."

"Oh, no?" Lisa asked innocently. "I think I can ride her better now."

"Really?" Brendan looked doubtful.

"I would like to try," she said.

Brendan lifted his hands, palms up. "It's your decision, but don't say I didn't warn you. You're sure the concussion is healed?"

"A-okay," Lisa assured him.

Russ interrupted. "Now, if you two will cut out the chitchat, Lisa can finish her breakfast and you can get there and be home at a reasonable hour."

Lisa quickly drank the rest of her orange juice. "Give

me five minutes to change," she told Brendan on her way to the bedroom.

She emerged after the allotted time wearing her faded jeans and a blue oxford-cloth blouse. She carried a yellow poplin jacket. The weather threatened to turn cooler in the evening and she wanted to be prepared.

Had she been able to foresee the next few hours, she would have known there was no way she could possibly have been prepared for the events to come.

CHAPTER EIGHT

Brendan eased the Jeep to a crunching stop on the gravel road. The trailer behind jolted lightly when they stopped.

"This is where the trail to the cabin starts," Brendan told Lisa. He glanced outside his open window toward the sky. The day had promised to be cloudy, and here in the highlands the clouds seemed to be grayer, thicker, and closer to the treetops.

"We may be in for some rain," Brendan observed with a glance at Lisa. "Are you sure you want to go ahead with this?"

"As sure as I can be," Lisa said. Her blue eyes met his gaze confidently. She wanted to show him that she wasn't the incompetent city girl he now took her to be. Suddenly it was very important that he think the best of her, rain or no rain on the horizon.

"Whatever your pleasure," Brendan agreed as he opened his car door and swung his long, booted legs to the ground. Lisa quickly got out of the car to join him.

He unloaded the two horses, talking softly to them as they clomped down the wooden ramp. Lisa slipped a sugar cube to Golden Girl, then gave her another one just for good measure. "Think of it as bribery," she whispered to the horse as Brendan retrieved their saddles from inside the van.

Astride Flyaway and Golden Girl, the couple headed up a narrow path, with Brendan in the lead. Their picnic

142

basket was secured to the saddle horn and hung along-side.

Every few minutes Brendan glanced behind him to check on Lisa and Golden Girl.

"Don't worry . . . we're fine," Lisa assured him after the fifth such check. She ducked to avoid an overhanging branch, one of many in these deep woods.

"I can see that," Brendan replied. "You look a lot more relaxed on her now. What gives?"

"Let's just say Golden Girl and I have come to an understanding," Lisa answered, laughing.

They approached level ground and a clearing. Lisa could not resist the urge to show Brendan how much she had come to terms with the horse. She clicked her heels to the filly's flanks, leaning forward, and cantered past Brendan. She glanced behind just in time to see the star-tled look on his face as she sped by.

"Giddyup!" He was coming up fast beside her on Fly-away.

Laughing, she shouted to him, "I was getting hot just walking, so was Golden Girl!"

Brendan grinned. "And here I was trying to take it easy on the city slicker! You must have been busy while I was away!"

Lisa nodded and slowed Golden Girl to a steady trot as they entered the woods once again.

"Russ was nice enough to help. He's a good teacher."

"Better than me, I can see," Brendan noted without a trace of rancor.

"Not—" Lisa's words were smothered by a sudden crack of thunder. Golden Girl started skittishly, and Lisa steadied her with a gentle but firm hand on the reins. "Whoa, girl."

She looked up nervously. Above the treetops the sky had darkened to the color of wet shale rock. Several drops of rain touched Lisa's face.

Brendan, who had guided Flyaway to follow Golden Girl on the path, was looking worriedly at the thick gray clouds overhead.

"Damn!" he said under his breath. "The cabin isn't much farther. Let's hope we make it there before the storm breaks."

The words were barely out of his mouth when another crack of thunder sounded in the still afternoon. Rain began to fall in earnest now, and Lisa tasted its wet arrival. She grabbed her jacket, which was rolled up behind the saddle, and struggled into it while keeping a one-handed grip on her horse's reins.

The air, which had been still for much of the day, suddenly came to life as the storm roared in. Gusts of wind whipped through the trees, shaking branches and whirling fallen leaves as if to rid them of their lethargy.

Golden Girl skittered in fright as a tree branch crashed onto the path behind them, just missing her hindquarters. "Easy, girl," Lisa soothed, patting her hand on the horse's neck. "It's going to be okay."

She wished she were as confident as her words indicated. The rain was slashing down in relentless fury now. It struck with bullet-fast speed on her face and body. Her jacket offered some protection, but not enough. And as the wetness soaked through her, she shivered.

Brendan rode up alongside her and, reaching over, gave her forearm a reassuring squeeze.

"You're doing great!" he told her, his voice fighting to be heard above the thunder and the wind swooshing through the trees. "Just a little while longer!"

He too was soaked to the skin. Without benefit of a jacket, he nevertheless seemed to Lisa to be impervious to nature's wrath. His shirt was soaked and molded to his chest, his muscles tense under the strain of holding Flyaway in check. Water streamed down his face and neck. It seemed to Lisa that his uniquely chiseled features were

144

even more defined; like the faces carved on Mount Rushmore, his was set in hard, timeless lines. Framing it, his hair was wildly curly, springing into tight coils with the onslaught of the storm.

He pointed to an obvious landmark, a white boulder that rose unmistakably in the center of the trail, which forked at that point.

"Just a few minutes and we're there. Can you hang on?" he shouted.

Lisa nodded, squeezing her eyes shut momentarily against the sting of the driving rain.

Brendan took the lead and Lisa followed. They veered to the narrow path that headed off to their right. It was muddy, and several times Golden Girl's hooves slipped in the wet muck and she stumbled. Lisa gripped her flanks as hard as she could with her legs, and hung on grimly. Her fingers and toes were numb and shivers racked her body.

Me and my bright ideas, she thought miserably. If this is what the country life had to offer, she would gladly regress to being a city girl.

She looked up to see a low L-shaped building of rough-hewn cedar in the clearing ahead. The cabin, at last! She nodded her head in happy acknowledgment when Brendan glanced back at her. Thank God they were finally here. She had even begun to doubt the cabin's existence while on the trail. Even now she hoped it wasn't merely a mirage, as water is to someone stranded on a desert, or as a rescue ship would be to someone floundering on a life raft.

The horses did not have to be urged to the overhang that served as their shelter. Brendan was off Flyaway in a flash and he stood beside Golden Girl as Lisa, with great effort, swung off the saddle. She half jumped, half fell into his waiting arms. Their sodden clothes made brief con-

145

tact as another crack of thunder sounded, this time closer and louder.

Brendan hurriedly tied the horses to the hitching rail and Lisa helped uncinch the saddles. She grabbed Golden Girl's saddle and, with a Herculean effort, managed to lift it off the horse. Stumbling under its weight, she lugged it to the porch. Brendan had done the same with Flyaway's saddle; the picnic basket still hung somewhat forlornly from the saddle horn, forgotten in the suddenness of the storm. Saddle blankets came next.

Brendan took Lisa's hand and together they made a dash for the front door of the cabin. In the growing dusk and fierce rain, she could not make out much more than a vague outline of her surroundings. She surmised that this was a no-nonsense cabin, equipped with few of the luxuries. She was right.

Brendan inserted a key into the lock and the pair stumbled inside. Lisa's eyes, unaccustomed to the darkness, could see nothing but hulking shapes and shadowy forms, objects she assumed to be furniture.

Brendan, familiar with the cabin's layout, moved swiftly. His boots made harsh, clomping sounds as the heels struck the hardwood floor.

He struck a match to ignite a gas lantern that rested on the hearth of the gray fieldstone fireplace. The gas mantle made a sharp, hissing sound as the flame caught and burned. Lisa watched as Brendan strode toward a far corner and lit another gas lantern. He glanced back toward Lisa, who stood shivering just inside the doorway. Small puddles of rainwater formed beside her sodden boots as droplets fell off her clothes onto the floor.

"You okay, Lisa?" Brendan looked worried. It *was* a hellish storm, and they seemed to have caught the brunt of its force.

Lisa nodded mutely, wrapping her arms tighter about

146

herself in an attempt to still the shivers that racked her frame.

Brendan busied himself tossing a supply of wood into the fireplace. "I'll have us warm in no time," he assured her. "Come over here by the fire."

Lisa did as he said.

"The first thing is to get you out of those wet things before you catch pneumonia," he said. Matter-of-factly, he began unbuttoning her poplin jacket.

Lisa stood perfectly still as his hands went about their work. Her own fingers were numb and frozen and were not much use to her. And Brendan was doing quite a capable job of ridding her of her layers of clothing. As if he had been undressing her on a regular basis, Lisa thought.

Anxious to erase that thought, she kicked off her boots as he was taking off her jacket. The red knee-socks that had seemed so snug and warm when she had put them on that morning were soaked through with water. They hung on her like lead weights. She rolled them down her legs and off her feet.

It didn't seem possible, but the rain had invaded everything she wore, down to her bra and panties, and the clothing hugged her body like damp wisps of nothing.

Brendan indicated her blouse. "Perhaps you'd be more comfortable if you took the rest off yourself. You can use the bedroom for privacy." His eyes were solemn, direct. "There's a blanket on the bed in there. You can wrap it around you. And bring your clothes out. We'll dry them in front of the fire."

Lisa hurried toward the door he pointed to, lantern in hand. Inside, her trembling fingers unfastened the buttons of her oxford-cloth shirt. She unsnapped her jeans, unzipped them, and peeled the wet denim down her bare legs. Underthings went next. She wrapped all her clothes in a bundle and found the blanket.

Her hand, poised to pick up the blanket and wrap its enveloping warmth about her nakedness, instead rested briefly on its folds. She spotted a closet door. She held the gas lantern high in front of her and walked over to find a red-and-black plaid flannel shirt hanging on a hook inside the door. It was the only piece of clothing in the room.

Quickly she reached up and snatched it off the hook. She slid her arms into the too-long sleeves, rolling up the cuffs until her hands appeared. She fastened the front buttons awkwardly as her still-cold fingers fought the unaccustomed left-side buttons on a man's shirt.

Mission accomplished, she looked down at the shirt-tails. They stopped midway between her hips and her knees. It wasn't the most modest outfit she had ever worn, but then it was an improvement on the blanket as adequate cover.

She stepped out of the bedroom, carrying her clothes to dry by the fire. Brendan was not in front of the fire, as she had expected. She heard rattling from a room she assumed to be the kitchen. She settled down on one of two big pillows that had been dragged before the fireplace and placed atop a sheepskin rug.

Brendan appeared then with two steaming mugs in his hands. He too had stripped off his wet clothes. He had found a beach-size towel, which was wrapped around his waist and secured with a knot. His chest was bare. Lisa tried and failed not to notice how his tanned skin gleamed in the flickering light cast by the fire.

He handed one of the large stoneware mugs to her. "It's hot buttered rum . . . almost as effective as a roaring fire to take the chill off."

Gratefully, Lisa wrapped her stiff fingers around the cup, letting the steam rise to warm her face. She sipped slowly, enjoying the warming effect of the hot liquid as it coursed down her throat.

Brendan noticed her attire. "I'd forgotten that shirt

148

was here," he said, looking down at her. "Mind if I join you?" Without waiting for her answer, he settled down onto the pillow beside her, stretching his long legs beside the hearth.

Lisa glanced about her. "Do you come here often?" she asked.

He shrugged. "When the mood strikes. I come here to think, sorting things out, mostly. No distractions, as you may have noticed."

He leaned closer toward her, and his chocolate-brown eyes sought hers. His lips parted. "No distractions, that is, until this moment." He took the mug of rum from her hand.

His fingers reached up to touch her chin. Ever so gently, his lips touched hers. Then his mouth parted from hers only to return an instant later with another kiss, more insistent than the last and creating an insatiable longing for the next.

Lisa pulled back. She ached to kiss him and keep on kissing him until the end of the world, knowing she mustn't. This was Brendan Donovan. Celebrity. Athlete. Ladies' man. Womanizer. Thief of hearts, breaker of promises.

"Lisa . . ." Her name on his lips sounded like temptation's whisper. His hands caught her arms and traveled to her shoulders, holding her in his grip as if determined that she feel the force of his desire.

She stared back at him. No words came. She was distantly conscious of the storm that raged outside. She was painfully aware of a closer, more turbulent storm, the one that raged within her heart.

He spoke for both of them. "Wanting someone . . . from the moment you first lay eyes on her . . . Lisa, Lisa, this is right. I knew it the first time. I'm sure of it now. You. Me. *Us.*" His words were more powerful than his caress.

Lisa gasped for breath. She felt as if she were floundering in a tumultuous sea and he was her anchor.

She did not know where the words finally came from except perhaps the depths of her soul. She heard herself saying, "Yes, yes . . . of course . . ."

To her surprise, she found herself reaching to touch his curly hair at his nape. Leaning forward slightly, she locked her hands behind his head.

They pressed together, mouths hungry for the nourishment to be found in the other's lips. His tongue explored the soft outline of her lips, the sharp edges of her teeth.

Lisa trembled, knowing that it was not from the wetness of the rain but from the moist desire that rose from the passion within her.

She felt at the same time helpless and invincible. Helpless, in that Brendan's kisses could melt away her resolve and reduce her to this limitless hunger for more of him. Yet she was invincible too, as if all that happened in the outside world could not possibly touch her here, in this secret inner world where the only thing that mattered was Brendan's touch.

Brendan caught her thick hair in his brawny hands, caressing her cheek as he kissed her. He groaned softly. "Tell me, Lisa, tell me . . . you want me as much as I want you. . . ."

Lisa needed no time to think. Here was her lifeline in the stormy sea, and she grabbed it. "Yes," she whispered. "Yes."

For a moment they were suspended in time and place. Her eyes met his, communicating in their depths what no words could express. Unblinking, unmoving, they stared at each other. Then, in unison, they followed this unspoken language that was as ancient as the earth yet still as new and different to them as a fresh spring flower.

Brendan reached out, his face now inches from hers, and his fingers tugged at the top button of the shirt she wore. His mouth sought hers again as his fingers continued down the front of the shirt. This small task done, his fingers touched her throat, traced lightly down to the valley between her breasts, to the blanket still wrapped about her hips.

Her hands trembled as she helped Brendan unfasten the buttons of her shirt. She arched her back toward him and at the same time her flesh nestled in the soft warmth of the sheepskin rug.

Brendan's kisses matched the heat of the fire, and her passion flamed and crackled as if a million tiny embers burned. He drew her still closer and eased her down to lie beside him on the rug.

His hands deftly explored her as his tongue sought hers and his mouth claimed hers. She placed the palms of her hands on the massive smoothness of his shoulders, caressing the marble-hard muscles that flexed beneath her touch as he reached to discover her hidden places.

His fingers touched her thigh, lightly rubbing her skin until she moaned with pleasure. Her touch found the compact muscles of his stomach and moved to explore his chest. He had aroused in her passion that was wild and free, lashing out against restraints.

Lisa returned his kisses with a ferocity that came unbidden. As his callused hands moved tantalizingly along her hips, she found in herself a delicious rhythm that matched his movements. At last his fingers touched her breasts, caressing her nipples until she cried out with pleasure.

She arched toward him, fitting her curves along his pantherlike leanness. He kissed her mouth, her eyelids, the soft hollows of her shoulders. She gasped as his lips moved to her breasts, as his tongue circled the pink tips. No thoughts intruded, save for the desire that this time would exist forever.

When his caress at last found the center of her passion,

151

Lisa abandoned herself to the wonderful maleness that was him. They pressed together, their mutual desire throbbing to become one. The flame, fed with yearning, licked at the heights in an ever-raging inferno.

Brendan reached impatiently for the towel that still encircled his waist. It came away like so much dust in his powerful hands. Lisa moaned as he pressed himself against her once more, and suddenly they were together, merged in a symphony of passion. His lips possessed hers with a fierce craving that she answered with her own.

"I love you," she whispered.

She had not meant to say the words. But they were so powerfully insistent within her, it was as if they were spoken of their own accord.

Brendan's hands cupped her face. His eyes searched hers for . . . what?

Lisa was suddenly aware that she had stopped breathing, as if she couldn't bear to take the next breath until she heard his response.

It wasn't long in coming.

"Lisa," Brendan whispered, "Lisa, my love . . ."

It was all she needed to hear. She kissed him then with all the pent-up desire that had been building to a crescendo within her since that first time on the riverbank.

She thought her longing could not be matched, but she was wrong. So wrong. Brendan responded like a man who has been released from the bonds of propriety, like a man who has rediscovered the primitive urges so long suppressed.

He gave everything in his lovemaking, and what he took in return was her heart.

CHAPTER NINE

Lisa awoke as the morning sun streamed in the window and made a patchwork of light on her bedspread. For a moment she could not remember where she was. The day before yesterday, in the cabin . . .

But this was two days later. She was in her bedroom at Brendan's house on Hilton Head Island. Alone.

She turned her head on the pillow to see the alarm clock on the bedside table. Ten o'clock. Late to be getting out of bed, but then the trip to and from the mountain cabin had been more than she had bargained for. In more ways than one.

But she had no time just now to dwell on those events. She and Brendan had left the cabin the next morning, after Brendan had made arrangements for a local handyman to make the minor repairs to the cabin roof that Russ had spoken of.

Upon their return that afternoon to Hilton Head, a message had been waiting for Lisa. It was from her editor, Marge Kent. She had returned the call immediately and heard the sobering news. The editorial schedule had been altered and the article on Brendan Donovan was scheduled for several weeks earlier than originally planned. Lisa was expected to complete the article within five weeks instead of the eight weeks originally allowed.

Lisa had hung up the telephone and taken a deep breath. And then took another one. Her deadline loomed impossibly large in front of her. She had no more time to wait for Brendan to overcome his reluctance to discuss Guy Tremaine or DEC or his rumored return to the racing scene. Thank heavens Marge had given her a few leads on those angles. Lisa had quickly made several long-distance phone calls, charging them to her credit card. She intended to follow them up with more calls once she returned to New York.

Perhaps, she thought now, the stepped-up schedule was actually for the best. She wasn't sure she could interview Brendan now, face-to-face, on a purely journalistic level. She would examine his face for clues and see instead the features of the man who had made love to her with such fierce passion.

Writing the article was another matter. She felt confident that when it came time to put words down on paper, her journalism skills would take over. She would be physically separated from Brendan then, so she could concentrate on her work to the exclusion of her personal feelings. It was more important than ever that she present an accurate portrait of Brendan. And now she knew him on the most intimate level possible. She longed to explore this newfound intimacy, but there was no time. She was due back in New York tomorrow, which meant she had to complete the first leg of her journey today.

But first she would meet Brendan on the beach, as they had arranged the evening before. Before going to bed, she had told him about the call from Marge Kent, the urgency of her deadline, and that she would have to return to New York to complete the article.

The disappointment in his eyes had told her everything she needed to know. Brendan had tried to persuade her to stay at Hilton Head and write the story there, where they could be together. Reluctantly, Lisa had refused. She explained that she needed to distance herself from him in order to do an accurate reporting job. She wasn't sure if he understood, but he did not argue with her decision.

But now as she got out of bed, she realized that these few hours at the beach would be her last with Brendan before she had to leave. Who knew when she would see him again?

Quickly she dressed in her black maillot bathing suit and slipped on a pair of rubber thongs. She found her beach towel folded atop her packed suitcase.

She encountered Russ in the kitchen, who told her that Brendan was already at the beach.

Lisa hurried along the trail leading to the beach, the pine needles crunching beneath her feet. She reached the sand at last and spotted Brendan, a solitary figure sitting just beyond the dunes, staring out to sea.

She removed her thongs and walked toward him. Her bare feet kicked up bits of sand as they sank in its warm cushion. Oh, how she would miss the island when she was in New York preparing to bundle up against the chill autumn air.

Brendan must have sensed her presence, for he turned to greet her just as she reached his towel. As if reading her thoughts, he said, only half jokingly, "You're willing to give up this for cold, heartless Manhattan?"

Lisa stretched her towel out beside his and sat down. She smiled ruefully.

" 'Fraid so. Because if I don't, Manhattan will be even more cold and heartless for one out-of-work writer. There isn't much demand for writers who fail to turn in assigned articles on deadline."

"I don't suppose there is." Brendan regarded her with a somber expression. He took her hand in his. "But you know, there is most certainly demand for the *other* L. B. Taylor."

"The other . . . ?" Lisa questioned falteringly. She felt her hand tremble ever so slightly beneath his touch.

"Yes," he told her in a voice that was tender. "The one who rides horseback in the mountains . . . the one who makes love like there's no tomorrow . . . the one who can make a man forget he ever looked at another woman . . . *that* L. B. Taylor."

He leaned over and kissed her. His lips, like soft feathers tickling her skin, tasted ever so faintly of salt from the sea.

Lisa was the first to pull away. "I'm not two different people," she whispered. "Just one person, who tries to keep her personal life separate from her professional life. Only this time I didn't succeed."

Brendan brought her hand to his lips and kissed the tips of her fingers, all the while holding her eyes with his own hypnotic gaze.

"Are you sorry that you weren't able to, this time?"

"Not . . . one . . . bit." Lisa fought to maintain her concentration as his other hand encircled her waist.

"What happens now, Lisa?" His mouth brushed her ear, sending shivers of delicious longing up and down her spine. "You go back to the city, write your story . . . and then what? When will I see you again?"

They were precisely the words she had wanted to hear, but she had no answer. "I . . . I don't know," she said. She wanted to tell him she would see him whenever, wherever he wanted. She wanted to tell him that her heart told her to stay here, with him, forever, and forget about her career. But something held her back.

Brendan released her. He leaned back, his elbows digging into the sand. "The articles you write," he began. "I suppose they take you all over the country, doing research and interviewing people?"

"Sometimes," Lisa told him. "The more well-known my work becomes, the more I get my pick of assignments."

She met his gaze and took a deep breath. "If *Lifestyle*

156

likes my profile of you, for instance, I should take a big leap upward on the totem pole of free-lance writers."

"And will they like it?" His tone was challenging.

"If I work hard on it, and make sure it's the best I can possibly do . . . *maybe* they'll like it." Lisa smiled.

"We never had that last scheduled interview," Brendan reminded her. "Will that be a problem for you?"

Lisa bit her lower lip, pausing to choose her next words carefully. "I don't think so . . . unless you planned to shed some light on a few remaining mysteries."

Brendan sighed. "You never give up, do you, Lisa?" The tenderness in his voice had been replaced by a wary coolness. "As I've already explained, I have good reasons for not wanting to discuss certain matters for publication."

"Then you won't tell me anything more about Guy Tremaine . . . about his expensive rehabilitation in a Paris hospital . . . paid for by a certain former race car driver?"

Brendan's brown eyes smoldered as he heard her words. He said through tightly clenched teeth, "Where did you come by that information?"

"Reliable sources," Lisa said noncommittally, in the same matter-of-fact tone that she used with all interviewees. "It wasn't all that difficult, Brendan. When you're a worldwide celebrity, people make note of your comings and goings. Paris isn't such a big city."

"Life in the fishbowl," Brendan replied gloomily.

"I thought you liked the recognition," Lisa countered.

Brendan sat up and reached for her hand. "Not when it interferes with my private life." He continued, "Lisa, I want to ask a favor of you. Don't include the part about Guy in the hospital in your article." His tone was earnest.

Lisa shook her head. "I can't promise that, Brendan. I wouldn't be any kind of journalist if I did."

"Maybe not. But is that more important to you than the fact that we're friends . . . very *close* friends? And you know as well as I do we've gone way beyond friendship, Lisa. Doesn't that mean more to you than a byline?"

"Of course our relationship is important to me!" Lisa replied heatedly. "But you can't ask me to choose between doing my job properly and answering to your wishes. It's unfair!"

"But if you really want to be fair, Lisa, you wouldn't pursue the Guy Tremaine angle." He paused. "Look, I'll be honest with you. Guy is undergoing rehabilitation at the *Institut Français* in Paris. In fact, he's due to be released very soon. And your source was correct. I paid for most of the treatment because Guy's insurance was woefully insufficient. But, my God, Lisa, it was the least I could do after the accident! And yes, I *am* helping him get started in business now that his racing days are over. But that isn't worth putting in your article, not when it will damage Guy's self-esteem. Hell, Lisa, the man's body *and* mind have been through torture over the last twelve months."

He took a deep breath, and when he spoke again, his words were carefully measured. "Bringing all this up in a publication like *Lifestyle,* with its millions of readers, well, I know Guy would be humiliated."

"How can you be so certain?" challenged Lisa.

"Because I know him. Already he's made a few references to himself as a 'charity case,' for God's sake. Write it up in your article, and the whole world might pity him. That's the last thing he wants or needs."

Brendan picked up a handful of sand and let it sift between his fingers. "Guy has a terrific mind, Lisa, that's what was behind all his racing trophies. He'll put it to use in business with me. I'm lucky to have him on board, but he doesn't see it that way . . . yet. And if your article comes out with his situation detailed for all to read . . . well, don't you see?"

Lisa nodded. "It is a slightly delicate situation, Brendan, as you describe it. And I'm glad you told me your side of it."

"My *side* of it!" Brendan exclaimed. "There's no 'side' to it but one . . . the right one. You won't ruin a man's future to further your own . . . or would you?" His eyes had narrowed and were regarding Lisa questioningly.

"Of course not, Brendan," she shot back, hurt that he would think such a thing. "It's just that I learned a long time ago to wait till all the evidence was in before I reached a verdict. The same holds true now, no matter who's arguing the case."

"Wonderful. You're a one-woman jury who'll judge the situation according to what your readers most want to hear about."

"As you so pointedly indicated when we began our interview," Lisa replied acidly. She fought to hold back tears that threatened to spill. His words cut deeply. Didn't he know her better than that? Was this all the respect he had for her chosen profession?

"And my opinion hasn't changed," he retorted.

Lisa stood up abruptly, holding her thongs in one hand. She yanked up her beach towel and bits of sand blew onto Brendan's bare legs. He ignored them, remaining stretched out, the length of his body covering his own beach towel.

"It's time I was on my way, Brendan," Lisa said. "I have a long drive ahead of me." She bit off the words.

"Should give you plenty of time to think about what I said."

"I'll do that." She fought to control her temper. This was not the kind of parting she had envisioned.

159

"Lisa . . ." Brendan stopped her, reaching up to grip her wrist. "We haven't talked about *us* . . . with you in New York, me here . . ."

Lisa disengaged her arm. She looked down at him with a troubled glance. "Maybe we had better wait till the article comes out, Brendan. You might not be too anxious to talk to me then. I hope you won't feel that way, but . . ."

Brendan stared at her. A muscle twitched in his cheek. "So you *are* going to write about Guy," he said at last, then shrugged. "It's your decision."

"Yes," said Lisa quietly. "It is."

A moment passed before either of them said anything.

"I guess this is good-bye, then, for now," Lisa said at last. The words were difficult to get out. She longed to forget all that had been said here this morning, and return instead to the cabin in the mountains where no differences came between them. But it was too late for that.

"I'll walk you back to the house." Effortlessly, Brendan hoisted himself up from his beach towel to stand beside her.

She started for the trail.

"Lisa." She stopped when he spoke her name. He was standing just behind her, so close she could feel his breath on her neck. His hand touched her lightly on one bare shoulder. As with the first time he had touched her, she felt her body come alive at the contact. She turned to meet his gaze.

"My feelings about the article . . . the things I said here this morning . . . that doesn't diminish what happened in the mountains and before. You were everything to me. The night meant something . . . very special to me. And I hope to you, too."

He kissed her full on the lips, their bodies not touching. His kiss had an air of finality to it that she could not mistake. Lisa pulled away. It took all her effort to keep

160

her chin from quivering, to keep the corners of her mouth upturned in what she hoped would pass for a smile.

"Yes," she agreed. "It did mean a great deal to me."

Did, as in past tense. But then she was only echoing his words. *It meant something special to me,* he had said. No mention now of any future between them, of any possible meeting. She had scotched that notion with her insistence on exploring the Guy Tremaine angle for her article.

Brendan thought she was merely a headline-grabbing journalist, like so many others he had encountered. He thought she was choosing her career over her feelings for him. And so, in his mind at least, their relationship would be confined to one rainy night in a secluded mountainside cabin and one night on a riverbank.

Lisa stood on tiptoe and kissed him, quickly. Her hand rested on his bare chest. Again she felt the unmistakable charge of electricity between them. Again she felt compelled to stay with him and ignore the consequences to her career.

But then her common sense asserted itself. The sooner she was gone, the sooner she could get on with the solid, dependable part of her life: her work. If she gave in to Brendan now, acquiescing to his wishes about the article, he would be happy for now. But how long would she be his love? A week, a month, who knew? His personal history wasn't noted for the longevity of his love affairs. And she would be left floundering, with no career to speak of.

Her work was the important thing, she reminded herself sternly. It was no substitute for love, but how dependable was Brendan's love, which seemed to hinge on agreeing to his demands?

She pulled away. Brendan Donovan was a finished chapter. His choice, she reminded herself grimly, not hers.

The highway stretched endlessly in front of her. Every mile she covered, every exit she passed, took her farther and farther away from the one man who meant everything to her. Still, she pressed her foot to the gas pedal and continued on the lonely road.

This early in the morning, on her second day of travel, she shared the highway with only a few other vehicles: trucks, mostly, a few businessmen in company cars, and the occasional station wagon loaded with family and vacation gear. They were brief encounters, passing by her, offering only a glimpse of other lives.

Lisa had never felt so alone in her life. She turned up the radio, hoping the songs and the deejay's chatter would offer company. But the noise only served to make her retreat deeper into her anguished self.

She had been alone many times before, but never so lonely. *Brendan, oh, Brendan, what have you done to me?* Lisa asked for what seemed like the hundredth time. She had spent the entire drive yesterday thinking of him. She had tossed and turned last night in her hotel room bed, trying and failing not to think of him and of the way his hands had so knowingly explored her flesh. And this morning, when she awoke, the first image that popped into her drowsy consciousness was Brendan's.

She was resigned to the fact that she would never get over him. Oh, there would be other men to date, maybe even a special one with whom she would someday plan a future. It wouldn't be Steve; she knew that her feelings for him had been a cheap imitation of love when compared with the real love she felt for Brendan.

Always, in the back of her mind, there would be Brendan.

The feel of his arms around her as they danced at Roulette. The tender concern in his eyes as he looked after her on the shores of the New River. The laughter in his

162

eyes as they shared a private joke. She would forget none of that.

She would cling to those precious memories, hold on tight until someday they slipped away, one by one, replaced by some dim recollection of the way it was. But she would never really forget.

Lisa glanced over on the bucket seat beside her. It held her briefcase full of notes and cassette tapes for her article. She touched it, as if by coming in contact with the rich brown leather she could draw some sort of strength. Within lay the artificial product of her few weeks with Brendan. Pencil jottings, snips of conversation, hastily scribbled notes in crowded margins . . .

Once these evidences of her profession had meant so much to her. Only yesterday, in fact, she had angered Brendan with her devotion to her writing. And what did she have today? Nothing but a briefcase, she thought sadly.

A small voice inside her argued that she was wrong to think that way. *You have your pride,* the voice reminded her.

She sat up straighter, accelerating just a little. *You're L. B. Taylor,* the voice continued. *You've worked for years to attain your career goals. Are you going to regret that because one man is so stubborn he refuses to listen to anyone else's point of view?*

The voice was one of the soldiers in the war raging inside her. It was a battle of emotions that seemed to drain all her energy. Clearly, the battle was a standoff. But it didn't matter which side won, she thought morosely. The spoils of this war were nonexistent. She wasn't likely to see Brendan Donovan ever again, except as a photograph in the pages of *Lifestyle.*

163

CHAPTER TEN

The *Lifestyle* profile on Brendan Donovan by L. B. Taylor attracted considerable attention. Not only was it the talk of the auto racing world, it was on the lips of celebrity-watchers in Europe as well as America.

Headlined WHAT MAKES DONOVAN RUN . . . AND RACE, the article went on to reveal that, contrary to rumors, Brendan Donovan had no plans to resume his career as a driver. He would, however, become heavily involved in promoting young drivers and new racing events, through the formation of a new company, Donovan Enterprises Corporation. Guy Tremaine would be its president. Tremaine's recovery was nothing short of miraculous and was helped in large part by Brendan Donovan's considerable financial assistance. But Donovan, the article said, was extremely reticent to discuss the issue of aid to Tremaine, because he was fearful that his appointment of Tremaine to his company's top post would be construed as a charitable gesture instead of, as he insisted, recognition of his friend's business talent.

Lisa looked up from the glossy magazine page and stared at the blank television screen in her apartment. She ought to feel elated, she knew, at the attention received by the Brendan Donovan profile. She ought to feel proud that her name was being bandied about in important publishing circles, and flattered at the telephone call she had received from a top literary agent who offered to

164

represent her for ten percent of the "absolutely wonderful fees you can command with the success of the Donovan piece, my dear."

But she felt none of those things. Instead, her mind kept returning to that last day at Hilton Head Island, on the beach with Brendan. She relived the conversation over and over again, first remembering the actual words that were exchanged, then changing the dialogue in a melancholy game of "what if?" so that their parting wasn't such a disaster.

What if, for instance, she had agreed to meet Brendan's request to ignore the Guy Tremaine aspect of her story? Or what if she had been able to convince Brendan of the unreasonableness of his position? Or what if, she mused wistfully, the topic had never surfaced at all and the two of them had spent their last hours together locked in unforgettable passion?

Unconsciously, Lisa wrapped her arms around herself, as if to simulate his touch. She longed to feel his masculine warmth flooding her senses, to hear his husky voice whisper tender words in the night.

In her mind's eye she saw him again as she had first seen him that night at Roulette—polished, tuxedoed, with an intoxicating charm that far outdistanced that of any other man in the place. She saw him too in the faded blue jeans and neatly pressed T-shirt that was his uniform at home on Hilton Head. He was all but unaware that those clothes defined him as finery could not; the tautness of well-trained muscles, the leanness of limbs tested to the limit—these were the disturbing images that floated in Lisa's mind.

She lifted a glass from the coffee table and slowly sipped her cola drink, savoring its flavor in the same way that she sought to savor her memories of Brendan. For that was all they were now. Memories. Hang on to them, she told herself, because—in the words of songwriter Paul Simon—they're all that's left you.

The telephone call, when it came, surprised her even though she had been half expecting it.

Brendan's voice on the other end of the connection sounded distant. His tone was no less so. "Congratulations," he said dryly. "I understand the article was a big hit."

"Thank you," she replied coolly, waiting for him to take the initiative.

After a short pause, he did so. "Your assumptions about DEC and Guy Tremaine were remarkably accurate, Lisa. I certainly can't fault you on that score."

"I assured you I would be accurate, Brendan. My by-line wouldn't be worth two cents if I wasn't."

"Hmmm. Always your by-line. I'm sure it wouldn't. As it is, I imagine you've dramatically improved your position in the world of sensationalist prose."

He said this so matter-of-factly that Lisa gasped. "Sensationalist! But you just said—"

Brendan calmly interrupted. "Accuracy, my dear girl, is no substitute for courtesy, which you lack in considerable abundance when it comes to your blasted career. I believe we covered the subject thoroughly in our last conversation."

"Not thoroughly enough!" Lisa stopped herself from shouting the words into the mouthpiece, even though she felt like it. The absolute gall of the man!

She continued, struggling to hide the frustration she felt. Her left hand gripped the receiver so tightly her knuckles turned white. "Just to clear the air between us, Brendan, you should know that I spoke to Guy himself after I returned here from Hilton Head. He verified most of what you told me, although, granted, that was very little."

166

"You . . . spoke with Guy?" Brendan sounded disbelieving.

"Like every reputable journalist," Lisa replied with sweet satisfaction, "I make it a point to talk to every possible source. He wasn't difficult to reach. And . . ." she added with relish, "he was very sensitive to my position."

"Was he, now," Brendan replied, waiting to hear more.

"In fact, he told me that he had heard the gossip himself—that you'd hired him for DEC because you felt guilty about the crash. He laughed it off. He's a tough man, Brendan. You should realize that," she added reproachfully.

Brendan answered testily, "He may act tough, Lisa, but inside he's still hurting. His doctors warned me that he cannot endure much stress at this point."

"Perhaps not," Lisa said. "But he's not averse to speaking the truth, as you seem to be. And he didn't regard me as a sensation-seeking journalist!"

Brendan laughed without mirth. "He'll learn. That'll be his first lesson as president of DEC—how to deal with the media."

"And you're the man to teach him?" Lisa asked incredulously.

"Lesson one will be not to get personally involved with any journalist."

Lisa heard his words and felt a sudden sick feeling in the pit of her stomach. Of all the angry words that had passed between them in this conversation, these were the most devastating to hear.

Standing there alone in her apartment, she fought for composure. "Good advice," she agreed, feeling a new tightness in her throat. It felt as if her heart had somehow pumped itself up and blocked her breathing. Every intake of air was a supreme effort. She scrawled meaningless designs on the scratch pad by the telephone as she took a

167

deep breath. "I'll have to remember that one myself, next time," she said.

There was a pause at the other end. Then Brendan's voice came through with deliberation, all emotion erased. "Yes, I hear you're in line to interview Senator Mark Aames. From what I hear, he has an eye for pretty female journalists."

"How . . . how did you hear I was assigned that piece?"

It had just been confirmed yesterday, Lisa remembered. News traveled fast, along routes you least expected, she thought.

"I spoke with Marge Kent today. She just happened to mention it."

Lisa wondered briefly what reason he might have had to talk with her editor. But the Senator Aames matter was foremost in her mind just now.

"Thanks for the warning," she replied sarcastically. The nerve of Brendan! Did he think she made a habit of falling in love with her interview subjects?

"Not at all," he answered smoothly. "And Lisa . . . another word of advice, if I may. I hear Aames is quite a sailor. Don't try to match him wave for wave. You do much better when you stick to what you *can* do."

"Don't be so sure of what I cannot do, Mr. Donovan." She resisted the urge to hang up on him. Instead, she added, "And you, Mr. Donovan, would do much better behind the wheel of one of your race cars . . . driving it in the opposite direction from me. Good-bye!"

She slammed down the receiver before he could reply. The force of her action assaulted her nerves. Not surprisingly, she found that she was shaking. She had had more than enough of his insufferable arrogance.

Why was it that every time she and Brendan talked to each other, the gulf between them widened to rival the

Grand Canyon? Now it was an unbridgeable chasm, so deep and wide she knew there was no getting across it.

And one of them didn't even *want* to cross it, she reminded herself. Brendan was content to regard their brief affair as past history. She smiled grimly at the irony of it. She had once regarded their affair in the same way. But the trip to the New River had changed that. For the first time, she had seen the man inside the public persona. She had seen a man who reveled in the camaraderie among friends, then a man who was concerned for her safety to the exclusion of all else. And, thanks to some insight from Guy Tremaine, she now knew that Brendan truly was reluctant about tooting his own horn in the pages of *Lifestyle;* she was sure that was one of the reasons he had been insistent about keeping his help to Guy such a secret.

Oh, it was no use. Why go on thinking about him? He was in South Carolina; she was in New York. And they were worlds apart in their thinking. Better to do something, anything, to take her mind off him if she could.

But what? The Aames series of interviews—five two-hour sessions, perhaps more if necessary—could not be scheduled until the senator returned from his fact-finding mission in Central America, three weeks from now. She glanced down at the scratch pad she had doodled on while talking to Brendan. In the middle of the meaningless scrawls she had sketched what looked like a raft. Subconsciously remembering the good times on the New River? Perhaps. But it jogged her memory and gave her an idea.

Wasn't there the basis of a story on ghost towns like Thurmond? For the first time since she had returned from Hilton Head, Lisa felt a smidgen of the old excitement that gripped her whenever the germ of a story took hold.

Ghost towns . . . legends . . . abandoned houses,

169

abandoned lives . . . wouldn't all that make for compelling reading in the pages of *Lifestyle?*

Lisa glanced at the phone, hoping for it to ring, hoping for Brendan to call and tell her it was all a misunderstanding. But she knew it wouldn't happen. She turned her back on it and headed for the typewriter. She would put Brendan out of her mind once and for all. She sat down in her chair at the kitchen table, hands poised above the typewriter keys.

She typed: *Article Proposal: Remembering a Town Called Thurmond.*

The Pines Motel was a good twenty miles from the ramshackle houses and empty dirt streets of Thurmond. The hotel manager, a talkative, diminutive woman whom Lisa guessed was either a spry seventy or a remarkable eighty years of age, gave her the key to room 104.

It was one of twenty-four rooms spread out in an L-shaped design beyond a gravel parking lot, in the middle of which was a separate, concrete-block building painted a bright orange and yellow. A blinking neon sign high above announced to passersby that EATS could be obtained within. Today a catfish special was advertised in the window.

A definitive aroma, not altogether appetizing, assailed Lisa's nostrils as she stepped outside the door of her room. Her car, this one a Ford compact rental car, stood in the slot marked "104." Not that it was vying for space. As far as Lisa could see, she was the only guest on this early Tuesday evening.

Lisa was almost tempted to sample the fish fry, aware that there was precious little else to do at The Pines Motel. A desultory playground, featuring one broken-down teeter-totter and a rusty swing set, didn't hold much appeal as the evening's entertainment.

Tomorrow she would begin making her rounds of

Thurmond's local historians, who might give her some background on the ghost town. Until then, she had time on her hands. She had to fill it, or be faced once again with thoughts of Brendan. She had successfully banished them thus far during her waking hours. It was only at night, when her mind refused to be harnessed by reality, that his face presented itself in her dreams.

She turned around to look inside her room. Her blue eyes strayed to the one double bed, covered in an old-fashioned white chenille spread, that dominated the small space. Would she dream of Brendan again tonight? Better to have nightmares about the spirits who supposedly inhabited Thurmond, she thought. That is, if The Pines Motel didn't crash down around her head during the night.

A trace of a smile played across her lips. The place was undoubtedly twice as old as the woman who had handed her the room key, and in not nearly as good condition. Paint peeled from a huge spot in the center of the ceiling. The carpeting was threadbare and the television, a tiny black-and-white model that Lisa guessed had made its debut right along with Uncle Miltie, refused to deliver anything but gray snow on its screen.

Maybe she could take that up with the manager. What was her name? Edna Purvis, that was it. If she could understand her, that is. During their initial conversation, Lisa recalled, she had had a hard time understanding the woman's thick West Virginia accent.

Numbskull! Mockingly, Lisa hit the heel of her palm against her forehead. Being a native West Virginian, Edna Purvis would probably know all about Thurmond! And she was right here at The Pines Motel, ready and hopefully willing to answer Lisa's questions.

She found the woman sitting in a rocking chair behind the front desk. She was engrossed in a copy of *People* magazine. At Lisa's entrance she looked up and shook her head, pursing her lips. "Says here that Liz Taylor had to be put in the hospital again," she said to Lisa. "She never shoulda divorced Richard, I don't care what they say."

"Er . . . I don't think they were very compatible," Lisa offered somewhat lamely in an effort to soothe the woman's obvious disappointment in the pair. If Edna Purvis, in her advanced years, kept informed on the very modern problems of Liz and Dick, could she be expected to fill her in on the ancient legends of Thurmond? Lisa was beginning to have her doubts.

Edna Purvis closed the magazine with a resounding *thwack.* She pushed herself up from her rocking chair, and Lisa noted that she was extremely agile for a woman her age.

"Yer thinkin' I'm gettin' outa this ol' chair pretty good, old as I am." Edna's frank words startled Lisa with their accuracy. She blushed scarlet.

"No need to be goin' all pink on me," the woman assured her in a thin, reedy voice. "They all do."

Edna laughed, making a sound that reminded Lisa of a frisky mule who has just outsmarted its masters. The wrinkles in her face became more defined, and behind her wire-rimmed glasses her gray eyes twinkled in glee. She scrutinized Lisa from her position behind the scarred counter of the front desk.

"Cain't say there's too many of 'em nowadays that do, 'cause we don't get too many payin' guests anymore. Just Cousin Seth and his brood o' heathens, but they're no-count 'cause they don't pay more'n a hill o' beans when they stay and the place is tore up for weeks after'n they leave."

She shook her head as if to rid herself of their bother. "Now, then, what can I do fer you?"

"Maybe a lot," Lisa began hesitantly. "I write for *Lifestyle* magazine . . ."

172

"Don't read that'un," Edna Purvis informed her quickly. "Too many rock stars on the cover. Who ever heard of callin' yerself the Doobies or some other name nobody can fit their tongue around, then dressin' up in tights, dyin' yer hair green—"

"I don't write about rock singers," Lisa broke in to assure her. "I'm here to write a story about Thurmond."

The elderly woman eyed her skeptically. "Why would anybody in his right mind want to write about Thurmond? 'Tain't nothin' but a ghost town."

"That's exactly why I am writing about it," Lisa told her. "You would be surprised at how many people are interested in ghost towns. Their history, why they're deserted now, the legends that have sprung up around them. Things like that."

Edna Purvis looked doubtfully at Lisa, worked her mouth a little, then noticed the notebook and pen in Lisa's hand.

"Yer not pullin' my leg?" she asked.

"Cross my heart."

"Well, shoot, most everybody around here has kin that lived in Thurmond. My granddaddy lived there, for a fact. Ernest Purvis. All the Purvises' first names start with an *E*. 'Cept for Seth, my third cousin—"

"Did Ernest work in the coal mines?" Lisa interrupted to get Edna back on track; she wanted to conclude the interview before midnight at the very least.

"That's right. Till they shut down. He worked right alongside a feller that claimed to be Adelaide Crawford's son. Granddaddy didn't know whether to believe him or not."

"Who was Adelaide Crawford?" Lisa prompted.

Edna blinked at her in surprise. "Yer writin' about Thurmond and you ain't heard tell of Adelaide? Why, shame on you, gal! She's about the best story ever to

173

come out of Thurmond. People say her story ain't done yet, neither."

Edna removed her spectacles for emphasis. Her gray eyes took on a visionary glaze. "Some people say you can hear her still at the entrance to Sunnyvale mine number three, cryin' for *him* to come out."

Lisa wrote quickly, anxious to capture the story as told by Edna Purvis. Adelaide Crawford lived in the mid-1800s. She was engaged to marry, but a week before her wedding day her Joseph was buried in a mine cave-in along with twelve other men. ("Thirteen," Edna pointed out, "see if that ain't an unlucky number.")

It seemed that Adelaide wouldn't believe that he was gone; she sat for days at the entrance to the mine, crying for her lover. One day the townspeople of Thurmond noticed her absence. Adelaide had disappeared, never to be seen again. Except, legend had it, at night when a ghostly presence wearing Adelaide's flowing white wedding gown would appear at the entrance to the mine, warning others away from the place. As for the man who claimed to be her son . . . well, speculation said that perhaps she and Joseph had jumped the gun, or so Edna Purvis said.

"Maybe," Lisa surmised. She glanced at her watch. "My goodness!" she exclaimed. "I've been here for over two hours. I didn't mean to monopolize your time."

"Don't fret." Edna patted her hand. "It's been a pleasure. Never been quoted in a magazine before. Remember, will you, that's Purvis, P-U-R-V-I-S."

Lisa laughed. "Thanks for your help."

She hadn't the heart to bring up the matter of the broken television set in her room. After all Edna Purvis had told her about Thurmond, she didn't need the diversion of television tonight after all.

The next afternoon Lisa set out in the Ford to see Luke Munroe. Edna had given her directions to the old man's

174

house, which was located at the end of a lonely stretch of road that had no name. Luke Munroe was acknowledged to be the local historian. If anyone could give her information about Thurmond, Edna had told her, it was Luke. Lisa had spent a rather fruitless morning tracking down other possibilities. She hoped Luke was the treasure chest of folklore Edna had built him up to be.

Lisa dressed for the weather. She had thought to bring a yellow rain slicker and umbrella in case of bad weather; the precaution had proven to be a wise one. She had awakened to the steady patter of raindrops on her hotel room window.

After eating a quick breakfast of hashed brown potatoes and orange juice at the diner—and enduring the frank appraisals of a pair of truck drivers—she headed for the car, using her umbrella as a shield against the heavy drizzle.

She followed the main road until she crossed the railroad tracks. A hundred yards or so past them, she turned left at the boarded-up general store. The road deteriorated to a series of potholes that had obviously been through too many winters untended. She drove cautiously, veering whenever possible to avoid doing even more damage to the shock absorbers of her rented car. The windshield wipers swatted rythmically at the rain.

Lisa checked the odometer. She had bounced along for five miles along this road. Eight miles to Luke's house, Edna had told her. When she saw the red arrow painted on a dead tree, she was to turn right. There were no road signs in this sparsely populated countryside; folks just asked around when they wanted to find someone, which was seldom, according to Edna.

Lisa wrapped her fingers tighter around the steering wheel as another rut nearly bounced her out of her seat. *Luke Munroe,* she thought, *I hope you have plenty to tell me about Thurmond's legends.*

She came to the tree with the red arrow, slowed the car, and turned right. The new road, if it could be called that, was certainly not listed on any Rand McNally map. Once it had been graveled and tarred, probably in the days when Thurmond was a thriving metropolis, Lisa guessed in jest. Now it was mostly dirt, interrupted here and there by outcroppings of weeds.

For a minute she wondered if she had followed Edna's directions properly. The woman had said the Munroe place was no more than ten minutes along this road. *I'll give myself fifteen minutes,* Lisa promised herself. If she hadn't found it by then, she would turn around and call it a day. The road was getting worse by the second, and the rain promised to make it slippery on her return.

From out of nowhere a brown dog of questionable parentage leaped to yap at the car's wheels. Lisa hit the brakes, thankful she wasn't going too fast or she might have run over the animal. For some crazy reason the dog reminded her of Flannagan, Brendan's Irish setter. She would miss that playful fellow . . . oh, damn, here she was doing it again. It was useless to think of Brendan.

She forced her mind back to the present. The dog looked well fed and cared for; he must be Luke Munroe's hound, Lisa figured, which meant she must be near the Munroe place.

She traveled a little farther. The white two-story house Edna had described stood some twenty yards off the road to her left. A red-haired old man sat alone on the front-porch swing, smoking a pipe. That's got to be Luke Munroe, Lisa thought. She gathered her notebook and pen for what she hoped would be an insightful hour or two.

It turned out to be four hours. By the time Lisa was through talking to the man, she wasn't sure just what kind of information she had because the interview had been a hellish one.

Luke Munroe, Edna had failed to warn her, had a

hearing loss. He didn't seem to recognize that fact, for he wore no hearing aid. Instead he would cup his hand around his ear and say, "Eh?" until Lisa shouted loud enough for him to hear her. Worse, he had a tendency to wander off the subject, so it was necessary for Lisa to steer him back to her questions at frequent intervals.

It was after eight o'clock, dark and still raining, by the time she got into her Ford for the trip back to The Pines Motel.

Lisa eased her car onto the road and peered out into the darkness. The car's headlights cut two swaths ahead of her, but in the unfamiliar surroundings they did little to help her navigate.

She spotted the turnoff road at last and swung the wheel. After she had gone several miles, she had to face the disturbing truth. She had turned down the wrong road by mistake.

"Blast it!" She pounded the steering wheel with her fist in frustration. The road was narrow and she was not sure what lay in the darkness on each side. It was impossible to turn around, so she would have to back the car down the lane.

She shifted gears and fixed her eyes on the rearview mirror. Slowly, slowly . . . good, she was going to make it out to the main road, if it could be called that.

She felt the left side of the car sink, as if going down a ditch. *Oh, no,* she prayed, *don't let it be what I think it is.* She gunned the motor, throwing the car into forward. If she couldn't go backward, maybe she could get out of it the way she had driven in.

No such luck. Lisa shifted from forward to reverse in rapid succession, and pressed down on the accelerator again. Nowhere. She was stuck.

She pulled her hood over her head and stepped out into at least six inches of gooey mud to investigate. This part of the road was a quagmire. The wheels were stuck,

177

that much she could tell with one quick look. Her efforts to extricate the car had only driven them deeper into the mud. Now it would take a tow truck to get the car out.

She looked desperately around her for any sign of civilization. No lights except her car's headlights and taillights were visible in the rainy gloom. The only sound to keep her company was the purring of her car engine and the whirring of the windshield wipers. And the rain, of course the rain. Why did it seem to thwart her at every turn? The trip to the cabin with Brendan, now this.

Lisa wanted to weep but forced herself to laugh instead, even though it came out more like a strangled sob. *I cannot cry,* she told herself; it would only add more water to the deluge.

She got back in the car and tried to think calmly. Her situation wasn't pleasant, but it wasn't disastrous either. Luke Munroe's place was probably closer than anything else out here. But how close Lisa wasn't sure. She realized that she had probably driven at least several miles and that his house was too far to walk to in this weather, at night and in unfamiliar countryside.

Well, perhaps someone would come down this road and find her before long. Any minute now, in fact. The thought was comforting but not very likely. Lisa suspected that whatever this road had once led to wasn't used anymore. Her chances of discovery were almost nonexistent.

That left one more option. She could resign herself to the fact that she was stranded here until daylight came and she could find her way to the Munroe place. The car was dry and relatively safe. Any prowlers out on a night like this, she thought, would be just as surprised at the sight of her as she would be to see them.

She wondered if Edna would notice her car's absence from the motel parking lot. If so, maybe she would send someone to look for her.

178

In the meantime, Lisa settled down to wait. She turned off the car's engine and lights and locked the doors. She removed her wet slicker, took off her mud-spattered boots, and curled up on the passenger side of the front seat, using her briefcase for a pillow. To pass the time, she mentally reviewed the information she had gathered thus far about Thurmond.

Her thoughts kept returning to the story of Adelaide. She couldn't stop herself from looking nervously out her car's windows, almost expecting to see the ghostly apparition in her white wedding gown. The slightest sound made Lisa jittery. She checked her watch again and again, waiting for daylight to come. She fell into a restless sleep sometime after 1:00 A.M.

The rapping on her window startled Lisa awake. Someone was outside the car. Lisa could make out the shape of a person's head and shoulders; it was a man, whose outline was barely illuminated by lights shining directly onto her car.

Lisa struggled upright and slid to the driver's side of the seat. Edna Purvis *had* noticed her absence and sent someone to find her!

She turned on her car lights to see better and rolled down the window. A voice in the darkness said wryly, "Care for a lift, or is this part of your research?"

That voice! Lisa thought she must be dreaming. For an instant the voice had sounded just like Brendan's. Impossible, of course. He was in South Carolina. He couldn't know she was here, wouldn't have any reason to be driving around the back roads in the middle of the night. Worse, Lisa thought, if he did know, he wouldn't care.

The man leaned forward and rested his elbows on her car door. As he did so, his face came into view by the light of the dashboard instruments. Lisa's eyes nearly popped from her head.

179

"How did you find me?" she managed in a faint whisper.

"With the help of a lady named Edna." Brendan smiled.

"But what are you—"

Brendan interrupted. "We can talk about that later. Right now I would like to get you out of this car and into my Jeep, so we can get out of this mud. If we stay here much longer, I'm afraid we'll both be stuck for good."

Lisa became aware of the rain, still coming down steadily from the black night sky.

She nodded her assent. "Just let me get my boots and raincoat on."

She busied herself as Brendan reached in, unlocked her car door, and opened it. He rolled the window back up and dashed the lights.

Lisa's mind was having trouble getting in gear. That Brendan was here in West Virginia seemed impossible. That he should be the one to come to her rescue was all the more incredible.

They hurried back to the Jeep, with Brendan carrying Lisa's umbrella and briefcase. The engine, which had been idling in wait, roared to life when Brendan shifted into reverse and gunned the motor to lift the wheels out of the mud's determined suction. Lisa watched him as he skillfully maneuvered the vehicle until they were out of the danger area and back on the right road.

Brendan wore a lightweight tan golf jacket, zippered over an open-necked denim shirt. The jacket and the jeans below it were thoroughly soaked. Lisa wondered how long Brendan had stood in the rain, tapping on her car window to rouse her from her sleep.

Brendan took his eyes from the road long enough to glance at her. "Are you okay?"

Lisa knew her expression must have been rather stupefied still. "Fine . . . perfectly fine," she answered.

180

"You and I seem to be getting caught in the rain a lot." Brendan chuckled. "I'm beginning to think we're to be first in line for Noah's next ark."

Lisa laughed at that, and the sound of it brought her to her senses. She shook her head to clear the cobwebs. "If I had known how bad the roads were to Luke Munroe's house, I never would have attempted to visit him in this rain," she confessed.

"Well, you couldn't have known," Brendan consoled her.

She looked at him sharply in the dim light of the Jeep's interior. Was this the same Brendan who had spoken so tersely to her on the telephone only a few short days ago? She wondered at the change in him.

They traveled along faster now, leaving a trail of muddy tire tracks behind. They would reach The Pines Motel in just a few minutes.

"I'm very grateful you came along," Lisa began hesitantly. "It was pretty spooky out there by myself."

"Glad to oblige a damsel in distress," Brendan replied lightly. He glanced at her and reached over, covering her hand in his.

"Now maybe we're even?"

"Even?" Lisa repeated, puzzled.

"That is, if you can forgive me for being an absolute mule about the *Lifestyle* article."

So that was it! Lisa suddenly felt as if she were soaring, her heart was so light.

Brendan was saying, "I realized after I talked with you that you hadn't done anything so terrible by writing about Guy and his position with DEC." He paused. "Well, that's not quite true. Russ made me realize it. He lit into me like he hasn't done since I was a kid. I guess he knocked some sense into me. Anyway, I apologize. You were only doing your job."

"Apology accepted," Lisa replied. She was almost

giddy at the nearness of him. She couldn't resist asking "But why bother to come all this way to tell me? You didn't have to."

Brendan laughed heartily. "Oh, didn't I? When I called your apartment and got no answer for several days, I called Marge Kent and managed to find out where you were."

His grin deepened, making creases in his familiar face. "Then once I heard the weather report for this part of West Virginia, I knew you were in deep, deep trouble. Now, a country girl could've handled it, but I knew a citified type like you . . ."

He playfully chucked her under the chin. His eyes teased hers.

"Would go to pieces," Lisa finished for him. She joined in his laughter.

Lisa held her hands up as if to surrender. "I give up trying to be the female answer to Marlin Perkins. I guess somebody other than me had better try to tame the wild kingdom . . . every time I try to make friends with the outdoors, it does its best to be my worst enemy!"

Brendan laughed as he pulled into the parking lot of The Pines Motel. Lisa was surprised to see lights still blazing in the office.

Brendan put the Jeep into park. "I'll just run in and tell Edna you're safe. She was worried about you."

He was back inside the Jeep in sixty seconds. "She said to tell you Luke Munroe has no more sense than a jack-ass to let you start out from his place so late and in such ripsnortin' weather. That's a direct quote."

Lisa grinned. "Sounds like Edna. If you'll park in front of room 104, you shouldn't get too much wetter. We'll make a dash for it . . . with the umbrella this time."

Brendan followed behind her. It was Lisa's turn to struggle to fit the key in the lock.

She switched on the light. "It's not much, but it's

182

home," she quipped. It seemed to be all she could think of to say.

They were like two strangers, she thought. Brendan stood in the middle of the small room, seemingly too large for its confines. Lisa made a big production out of taking off her wet boots and rain slicker. The room was deathly quiet, the air unusually still.

There didn't seem to be anywhere to sit but on the bed. Lisa perched on the edge of it, nervously smoothing the bedspread with her hand. She felt like a teen-ager on her first date.

"So . . ." she broke the silence. "I hear Donovan Enterprises Corporation is doing splendidly."

"As a matter of fact, it is. Especially since your article came out."

Staring at the floor so she wouldn't have to meet his eyes, Lisa said almost inaudibly, "I'm glad *something* benefited from the experience."

She still felt bruised and exhausted from the whole complicated affair. True, Brendan had apologized for his adamant opposition to the article's contents. But that didn't automatically transform their relationship back to the way it was before. She doubted if anything could.

Brendan's hand touched her shoulder. She looked up expectantly. With his other hand he pulled a tissue-wrapped object out of his rain-soaked jacket pocket. The rain hadn't penetrated to the tissue, luckily.

"I wanted you to have this." He placed it in her open palm and sat down so close beside her that his leg touched hers.

Carefully, Lisa unwrapped the flimsy white tissue. Whatever it was, the object weighed no more than a few pounds and was about the size of an orange.

She caught her first glimpse of smooth teakwood and her lips parted in surprise. It was a miniature carving,

183

done in Brendan's distinctive style, of a mallard, its detail and proportion superb.

"It's beautiful," she breathed.

"And it was inspired by you," Brendan added quietly. "I seemed to have a lot of time on my hands after you left, Lisa. I meant to work on a pelican carving I had promised to a friend of Russ's. Instead, I . . . came up with this. I hope you like it."

"I'll treasure it . . . always." Lisa's voice broke on the last word.

"Maybe you could pack it in your suitcase on your travels . . . sort of as a good-luck charm," Brendan suggested. The first hint of shyness that Lisa had ever heard from Brendan was present in his words. "I hear Senator Aames is one tough nut to crack."

Lisa looked sideways at him. He was so close she couldn't breathe all of a sudden. Or was that due to something else, some surging hope within her that maybe this wasn't the end after all?

"I will," Lisa promised. She stroked the carving absently, her mind filled with thoughts of the man beside her.

"It has a mate, you know." Brendan's breath tickled her ear. "A matching carving . . . almost finished." He hesitated. "You could pick it up on your next visit after you've finished with the Aames article and before Marge Kent assigns you to the next one. We could take another horseback ride, to the cabin."

"Yes," Lisa whispered, and held her breath. She still could not bring herself to look at him, as if doing so would break the spell. "Yes, we could do that."

"And afterward . . ." His lips brushed hers and Lisa closed her eyes. "Afterward, we'll—"

His unspoken suggestion was interrupted by a sharp knock on the door of the room. Lisa started. Who could that be? Brendan quickly crossed the room to find out. Lisa carefully placed her carving on the nightstand.

Edna Purvis stood on the doorstep. In her arms she carried a tray that held two chipped china cups. "I thought you two could use a hot toddy," she announced sweetly. Without waiting for their reaction, she walked into the motel room and placed the tray squarely atop the scarred walnut bureau.

She turned to Brendan. "Now then," she said briskly. "Would you be wantin' a room for the night?"

Lisa spoke quickly, instinctively. "No, he won't, Edna. He'll be staying with me."

She glanced with sudden shyness at Brendan. Their gazes locked. He spoke softly only to her. "Always."

They hardly noticed Edna's exit.

The hot toddies were forgotten as Lisa rose to stand before Brendan. She reached up and put her hands on his granite-hard shoulders.

"I'm so glad you came, Brendan." She stood on tiptoe and kissed him. "So glad . . ." she repeated, then stepped back and smiled.

"Why quit when you're ahead?" Brendan teased, reaching for her. He kissed her and his mouth lingered tantalizingly over the soft suppleness of her lips.

"Tell me," Lisa said after a moment, "what can I do to repay you for rescuing me out there tonight?" Her voice was husky and there was a provocative tone that couldn't be mistaken. Her blue eyes sparkled as she softly bit her lower lip.

Brendan's low, throaty laugh rumbled pleasantly in her ear. He whispered only to her, telling her exactly what she could do to thank him.

Lisa nodded and nibbled playfully on his earlobe, her fingers tracing the outline of his shoulder blades through the dampness of the jacket he still wore.

"The first thing I'll do is get you out of these wet

clothes," she said, easing the jacket from his broad shoulders.

Brendan swiveled his head ever so slightly, surveying the motel room. "What, no fireplace?" he said in mock dismay. "Guess I'll have to find some other way to get warm."

Lisa kissed him fleetingly and turned away. She walked across the room and flicked off the light switch, then locked the door. She went to the window and pulled the shade down, plunging the room into utter darkness. Brendan stayed where he was as she moved swiftly toward the tiny bathroom. She turned the switch on and light spilled out to the larger room. Lisa pulled the door partially closed so that only a sliver of light cut through the darkness. It was enough for them to see each other fully.

"Come here," Brendan demanded hoarsely.

Lisa glided into his arms, expecting them to enfold her. Instead, Brendan scooped her up, his grip powerful around her legs and shoulders. He carried her to the bed and gently lowered her so that her head rested on the pillow.

Brendan straightened and stood before her. Quickly he removed his shoes and socks. His right hand moved to the buttons of his shirt-sleeve cuffs, then down the front. In one fluid motion his shirt was off.

Lisa swallowed hard and looked up at him, her breathing coming in quick, shallow gasps.

Brendan unbuckled his belt and unzipped his jeans. He pulled the denim down over his slim hips and the jeans fell to the floor, making a faint thudding sound as they landed. He stood not more than a foot away from Lisa, clad only in the barest of briefs.

"Why quit when you're ahead?" Lisa asked in the softest of whispers. Brendan obliged by removing the last of his clothing.

186

"Your turn," he said, and moving to the bottom of the bed, slipped off Lisa's muddy shoes. Then he peeled off her knee-high stockings. He moved up the bed, balancing on his knees. Off came her slacks, then Brendan's hand caught her wrist and in one deft motion he unbuttoned the cuff. He did the same to the other. His fingers found the buttons at her neck and Lisa caught his eyes and held them as, one by one, he unfastened the buttons of her blouse. She shivered in delicious anticipation as his fingers skipped along her willing flesh.

This done, he stretched out on the other side of her and, before she knew what was happening, pulled her on top of him. Their noses were almost touching and she could feel his sweet, warm breath on her face. His lips were just a touch away, slightly parted, promising more.

With his two hands Brendan rolled the fabric of her blouse down her shoulders, down her arms, and off. The air hit her skin and goose bumps appeared on her arms.

Brendan, feeling her shiver, rubbed her arms with his callused hands, slowly, up and down, until she was so warm she wondered that she didn't melt. She thought she would perish if he didn't kiss her soon.

She could wait no longer for flesh to meet flesh. Quickly she reached behind her and unclasped her bra. She rose up and shrugged her shoulders so the straps fell down her arms. Brendan, his breathing coming at breakneck pace, grabbed impatiently at the wisp of sheer nylon and tossed it to the floor.

Lisa's lips discovered the hollows of his neck and her fingers, pinned beneath her, played at the silky hair that sprang from his chest.

"Oh . . . yes!" she moaned as Brendan slid his fingers beneath the satiny smoothness of her bikini panties. She was only vaguely aware of their removal as Brendan's mouth sought hers with abandoned passion.

"Lisa, Lisa," he whispered urgently as he kissed her

187

nose, her cheeks, her eyelids, her throat, and back again to the fullness of her lips, now swollen with wanting him. His hands were moving, moving to every place she wanted them, and her own fingers were finding the hard maleness of him.

"You don't know how much I love you, Lisa," Brendan breathed.

"I . . . think . . . I . . . do," Lisa said between kisses, each one longer than the last. She tore her mouth away from his for only an instant. "But maybe you should show me?"

"With pleasure, my love . . ."

And Brendan showed her, evoking more pleasure than Lisa had ever known before, yet not as much as she would begin to know with Brendan. She only knew that this was magic, so special it should have been make-believe, so wonderful that she was glad it was real, as real and true as their love.

Then Brendan whispered to her again and they traveled to a far, far place where only a fortunate few are privileged to enter.

Candlelight Ecstasy Romances™

$1.95 each